THE SECRET OF THE PIT

The Secret of the Pit

Hugh Scott

Hodder
Children's
Books

a division of Hodder Headline plc

**For my daughter, Caroline,
with all the love in the world**

Copyright © 1998 Hugh Scott

First published in Great Britain in 1998
by Hodder Children's Books

The right of Hugh Scott to be identified as the Author of
this Work has been asserted by him in accordance with
the Copyright, Designs and Patents Act 1988.

10 9 8 7 6 5 4 3 2 1

A Catalogue record for this book is available
from the British Library

ISBN 0 340 70435 7

Typeset by Avon Dataset Ltd, Bidford-on-Avon, Warks

Printed and bound in Great Britain by
Clays Ltd, St Ives plc

Hodder Children's Books
a division of Hodder Headline plc
338 Euston Road
London NW1 3BH

1

Somewhere in Scotland

My kids say to me, 'Dad, you *are* thick,' and I laugh.

I know they're joking.

I know from the look they give their mother, and she – Esther, that's their mother – my Esther – says, 'Don't be rude to your father!'

Then she'll knock their heads together (gently), and they'll rub their scalps and produce tears. What acting! What characters!

Josie came into the kitchen – she's thirteen – and said, 'A table for six has just come in, Dad. Hungry-looking lot.'

Well, I popped my head into the restaurant and sure enough three couples were shuffling around a table wondering where to put a woman in a wheel-chair.

I smiled to myself because, ha! ha! no way could Josie tell that these six were hungry; *I* reckoned Tea and Cakes, that's what I reckoned, which meant that Esther would cope; Esther being our waitress as well as my wife – with Josie, of course, helping, in order to earn herself a few pounds.

Frances is our other real waitress. She brings in the men customers.

Frances brings in the men customers because she's a sweet child, with hair like polished wood, which she clasps back to keep it from swinging into the soup. When I say 'child' I don't mean she's a child; she studied at college, but couldn't concentrate for falling in love, and became a waitress instead.

But I was saying about Josie guessing that these customers were hungry. No way! Tea and Cakes.

I ducked back into the kitchen. Half-past eleven. Too early for them to want lunch anyway.

I decided to blanch some chips so that I wasn't caught out, because workmen were digging up the pavement at Rose Cottage – I laughed – Rose Cottage! I ask you. Fancy calling your house Rose Cottage! 'Ho! Ho!' I chortled, and popped the chips into the frier and watched 'em descend automatically into the fat.

In four minutes the frier would lift the chips up, out of the fat, ready for a final cooking later, when the workmen arrived.

They like chips, workmen do.

I wondered where Jamie was. He likes chips. He's my youngest. Nine, he is, going on forty. Ha! Ha! Ha!

The kitchen door bumped open. 'Six large pizzas, Allan.' Esther smiled as she handed me the slip of paper with the order on it. She always smiles, does my wife. Nice woman. 'For the people with the wheelchair.'

She bumped out.

I was right – you can't tell if people are hungry;

I was *sure* they were Tea and Cakes.

Then in shoots Jamie, his little face as bright as butter, and he yells, 'Dad!' and I say, 'Ha! Ha! Jolly good, Jamie.'

'Listen, Dad!'

'Pass me six large pizza bases, son.' And he passes the bases from the fridge, and I splodge on sauce and smoked sausage and mushrooms—

I stopped, and looked at Jamie.

He was staring up at me, his mouth tight.

'What?' I asked.

'Are you listening?' he demanded.

'I always listen, Jamie. You know that. I always listen to everything you and Josie want to tell me—'

Jamie's eyebrows levelled over a frown.

I folded my arms.

'I really *am* listening,' I smiled.

'You're smiling.'

I blinked the smile away. What a child. Isn't he great?

4

'You know,' said Jamie, 'that the workmen are digging up the pavement? Guess what, Dad. They've found . . .'

I nodded carefully. Didn't want him to think I wasn't listening. The workmen were digging up the pavement outside Rose Cottage. The whole village knew that. Rose Cottage I thought. What a daft name . . .

'—!' said Jamie.

I stared at him.

'Well?' he demanded.

'Well . . .' I said, '. . . that's very interesting, son.'

'Interesting!'

I opened my mouth.

'Interesting!? MUM!' he bawled. He bumped out of the kitchen.

I heard Esther hushing him.

She said, 'What?'

Rumble, rumble, from Jamie.

'Did you tell your father?'

'He said it was interesting!'

5

'Interesting! I'll deal with him! You go and keep an eye on these workmen!'

When Esther bumped into the kitchen, I made sure I was busy with my six pizzas.

2

Esther towered beside me. Not over me, because she only comes up to my ear, but she certainly can tower. Now. I know that I missed what Jamie had told me, but it couldn't have been so vital that Esther towered . . .

She stood with her fists on her waist, a dish towel in one hand.

I raised my eyebrows at the pizzas, and skimmed two of them towards the pizza oven, but Esther stepped in front of me.

I smiled down on her, the pizzas on my palms.

'You won't listen to your own funeral service, will you!' she demanded.

'Probably not,' I beamed, and swung round her, sliding the pizzas on to the hot shelf in the oven, slipping them further in with the pizza shovel. I had slid the second two in before Esther towered again.

I lifted the last two pizzas.

'You didn't listen to Jamie!'

'I said it was interesting. I expect,' I soothed her, 'workmen are constantly digging up things which are interesting—'

'A sk- - - - - -,' hissed Esther. She has beautiful eyes. Fiery. Tough, is my Esther, and I love the way her hair hangs in dark flops around her face. But I hadn't caught what she'd said.

'A sk- - - - - -?' I repeated.

'A skeleton,' she agreed, 'just round the bend from this restaurant!'

My mouth opened.

A skeleton.

'You heard now, didn't you?'

'Dead?' I whispered.

Esther glared with her beautiful eyes.

I said, 'Oh,' and excused myself around my wife

and put the last two pizzas beside their chums in the oven.

Frances bumped into the kitchen.

'Bacon roll twice, please, Allan,' she whispered. 'For Lenny.' She stared moistly at me, blinked at Esther, then bumped out.

'Frances is looking a bit moist,' I said to Esther.

'Never mind Frances—!'

I laid bacon to frizzle on the hot-plate.

'I want you to listen to me, Allan!'

'I am listening, Esther,' and I stood looking over her head, my eyes seriously on the frying bacon. Two bacon rolls for Lenny. When he'd eaten those, he would order three more, one at a time. As strong as four navvies, is Lenny, but with a voice that breaks windows, and the IQ of a fried egg—

A dish towel cracked against my ear.

'Will you listen!'

'I am listening, Esther,' I assured my wife, and rubbed my ear.

Then I did listen.

I looked at her, and something in her face drew my whole attention. '. . . narrow,' she told me.

'Narrow?' I asked.

Esther leaned up close to me. She held her palms just far enough apart to hold, say, a four-kilo tub of *I Can't Believe It's Not Butter!* – though she wasn't holding anything.

'As narrow as that,' said Esther quietly, 'but it's not a child's skeleton—'

She was talking about the skeleton.

'Jamie told you this?'

'Yes, Allan. Jamie told me this. You know he's reliable.' Esther was speaking as if I were a child, too.

'Too narrow,' she murmured – she moved her palms on to my cheeks so that I had to look into her eyes. 'Too narrow for a human being, Allan. Do you understand?'

'An animal?' I suggested.

'Not an animal, and not a human being—'

I opened my mouth to laugh, but Esther's palms held me.

'Not a hoax, Allan—'

I tried to shrug. I mean – how does a child like Jamie know that a skeleton's not a hoax?

'The workmen have sent for the police—'

'Really?'

'—because they're nervous.'

Esther held me with her beautiful gaze. She let her palms slide off my cheeks.

I said nothing.

Nervous about what?

'The skeleton,' whispered Esther – and she smiled up at me as she spoke, for she knew that I had heard every word, 'has horns.'

3

Horns.

A skeleton with horns.

A sheep, obviously. But I didn't say anything. I stepped aside from Esther, and popped the bacon into the rolls. Esther took the rolls and bumped out of the kitchen, satisfied that I had understood what she'd said.

I heard Lenny's voice.

Not human.

I wondered where my Josie was. She hadn't reappeared since telling me about the six people with the wheelchair.

But not animal.

Josie – probably – was outside Rose Cottage waving her eyelashes at the workmen. Looks like

Esther, does Josie, with hair that flops, and the same eyes. Josie is a flirt. At thirteen.

Frances isn't.

I did say that Frances has hair like polished wood. In she bumped, Frances, and stared at me.

'They want their pizzas.'

We watched the pizzas in the oven until the cheese bubbled, then I slid them on to a tray and pushed the tray into Frances's hands.

She whispered, 'You take it.' She still looked moist.

I frowned and smiled.

'Please.'

Frances returned the tray to me, and her eyes stayed on mine as I backed out of the door, leaving her in the kitchen.

Esther was clearing Lenny's arms off his table so's she could put down a pot of tea. She gave me a look that told me she was still thinking about the skeleton.

The six people with the wheelchair were at the

fireside table, and one was lifting wood from the basket on the hearth, and stoking the flames. It wasn't a cold day; just cool enough for a fire to be welcoming. And they were wrapped up, these people, in hats, coats, gloves, with plenty more clothes under the coats. One woman had her hat on backwards. I think.

I think it was a woman.

I *had* thought – when I'd looked from the kitchen earlier – that they were three couples.

I smiled at them. Some wore men's trousers, but—

Three couples of what?

Their clothes didn't tell me, being somewhat mixed-up, with one bony face above a woman's fur collar.

I served the pizzas.

They smelled of mothballs. The six people, I mean.

I kept smiling. They smiled back without showing their teeth.

'Come far?' I chatted, glancing at the flames standing in the fireplace. Their faces were tanned. Spain, I reckoned.

'Thpain,' whispered the person in the wheelchair.

I usually chat more, but I didn't. Not with these people. Something was making the hair on my neck stand on end. I remembered Frances being moist in the kitchen, and excused myself.

I bumped in. Frances was rinsing her face at the sink. She dabbed her eyes on her apron. Her polished-wood hair (in its clasp) hung down her front. She swung it back, and tested her face with a smile. She'd been crying. She said, 'Allan . . .'

I raised my eyebrows.

'The people at the fire . . .'

'Yes?' I found some dirty dishes, and lifted them.

'Didn't you notice . . . ?'

'Spanish,' I assured her, and carried the dishes into the washing-up room.

'No,' said Frances in a distant voice. 'I don't think they're Spanish.'

I went back to Frances.

She said, 'I don't think—'

I wiped a work surface. 'Excuse me.' I reached past her, finding another surface to wipe.

Frances walked away. She stood at the kitchen door.

'You know you can tell me,' I said, still wiping.

'How?' whispered Frances, and the door swung, bumping, leaving me suddenly lonely.

I stopped wiping.

The hairs on my neck went on prickling.

Orders flowed in.

It was twelve o'clock and lunch-time. I hadn't had a chance to think about the skeleton. It had to be a hoax. Though how anyone planted it under the pavement, I couldn't guess, because the workmen had only started digging that morning. Probably some smart-Alec medical student, I reckoned – if most of the thing was human, with horns.

I laughed, 'Ho! Ho!' but Esther bumped through with an order, and I changed my laugh to a song. Amazing how things could be faked these days.

But, as I say, I didn't have time to think.

Then the lunch-time rush ended, except for the workmen, who – Josie dashed in to inform us – were delayed by the police, so I made myself haddock and chips.

Esther came in to take over the kitchen, and said something, but I was washing the smell of cooking off my face and didn't catch it. Then I discarded my apron to put on a jacket so that I looked like a customer, and sat in the restaurant at a table for two, which is the smallest size of table we have.

It's bad manners, I always think, for staff to eat among the customers, which is why I sort myself up. Of course our regulars know me, but they appreciate the effort.

Then the workmen came in, and policemen, shoulders filling the restaurant. The six people at the fire had gone. But Lenny was still pouring himself tea and demolishing his fifth bacon roll. He voiced a remark which ended with, '. . . CAKES,' and I smiled. He wouldn't know that I wasn't listening.

I dug into my fish and chips.

'. . . CAKES,' boomed Lenny, from his table, and he nodded at the cake display in our glass counter. I glanced, munching, at the display, then stopped munching.

The cake plates were empty except for crumbs.

I frowned round for Frances. She should have put more cakes on display. She zoomed past with the workmen's lunch orders and vanished into the kitchen.

The kitchen door swung and I glimpsed Esther, smiling as usual, but pale, and I caught her words to Frances: '. . . tried to tell Allan . . .' Bump, swing went the door. '. . . too busy washing his face to listen . . .'

I remembered she'd spoken when she came into

the kitchen to let me out for my lunch; maybe she'd mentioned cakes then.

'. . . FORTY-TWO CAKES,' said Lenny as Frances zoomed from the kitchen with fresh cakes. She filled the display.

'THE PEOPLE AT THE FIRE ATE FORTY-TWO CAKES.'

Frances – having already taken the workmen's order – approached the policemen with her pad poised, and suddenly – and quite gracefully – fainted.

4

Frances looked nice lying on the carpet.

The youngest policeman felt her pulse and tidied her hair off her face. One of the workmen volunteered the kiss of life.

I announced who I was, and everybody relaxed interestedly. Frances sat up, and I helped her to a corner table, then I asked Lenny to fetch Josie and Jamie from their observations of the pavement, and he ambled off, sucking bacon grease from his thumb.

I poured water for Frances to sip, and asked what was wrong.

'You can tell me,' I encouraged her. She turned her head towards the kitchen. 'Do you want Esther?' I asked.

'Oh, no. She's already worried about these people eating forty-two cakes. *Can* I tell you?'

'You know you can.'

'Oh, yes! But will you take it in?'

'Frances!'

'I'm sorry, Allan. But I . . . *poop! poop!*' That was her crying.

I patted her hand. The young policeman looked over. I mouthed, 'She's okay.'

'*Poop!*' sobbed Frances.

'Tell me what's wrong.'

'*Poop.* Those people, *poop!* at the fire. *Poop*, one in a wheelchair—'

'Spaniards,' I nodded.

'Oh, Allan . . .'

I hoped Josie and Jamie would arrive soon to get on with wiping tables and brushing carpets. I thought of the policemen waiting for their lunch orders to be taken. I wondered if anyone was guarding the bones outside Rose Cottage.

Rose Cottage. What a name for any man to give

his house. Though, of course, it wasn't a man. Mrs Patience lived in Rose Cottage. She'd been there as long as anybody knew—

'—!' gasped Frances. '*Poop poop poop poop—!*'

'Oh, really?' I said, patting her hand harder.

The young policeman laid his shadow over the table.

'Let me,' he said, so I let him take charge of Frances's hand while I took the other policemen's orders. Josie and Jamie shot in and asked what was up with Frances. Lenny, lumbering in with them, announced that, 'THEY ATE FORTY-TWO CAKES.'

I couldn't make head nor tail of all this.

I passed the lunch orders to Esther in the kitchen and returned to my own lunch, and thought.

I thought, What a morning! A skeleton dug up just round the corner from my restaurant. With horns.

Frances tells me why she fainted, but I don't listen.

And to crown it all, Lenny keeps saying that the

people at the fire ate forty-two cakes. I laughed into my haddock.

'BUT IT'S TRUE,' said Lenny, and I realised he had said it again. 'THEY ATE—'

'D'you want to pay?'

So I took his money and told him to keep an eye on the skeleton, and he said there was a policeman doing that until the doctor came.

I said, 'Oh,' and threw him out.

I went into the kitchen.

'Esther,' I said to my wife, 'you were trying to tell me something. You came in here all pale, but I was too busy washing my face to listen. I'm sorry.'

She stared at me, her hair flopping sweetly, then she said, 'The people at the fire ate forty-two cakes.' She continued staring. 'You heard that, didn't you?'

'Lenny kept saying—'

'They ate forty-two cakes,' repeated Esther. 'I had trouble keeping Lenny quiet. You know how he shows off his counting. I don't want foreigners embarrassed by lunatics making comments.'

'Forty-two?'

'Chomped them up and gulped them down. Are you still listening, Allan?'

'Yes—'

'It was frightening. Seven cakes each. Nobody can eat seven cakes. Especially after a large pizza. And they were such small people . . .'

'Were they small?'

'You saw them. You served them.'

'Spanish. Plenty of clothes—'

'They were small inside their clothes.'

'I noticed that,' I said. I had. I think I had.

'Have you finished eating?' Esther asked. She eyed my jacket. I didn't take it off.

I said, 'Is that why Frances fainted?'

'What!'

'She's okay,' I assured her. 'A policeman's holding her hand.'

'I thought there was something else on her mind. Didn't she say?'

'She did mention . . .' I shrugged.

Esther's mouth clamped itself shut.

I raised my eyebrows.

She shook her head making her hair flop angrily. She knew I hadn't listened.

I changed the subject. 'I'll be back in a few minutes,' I told Esther.

I bumped out of the kitchen, casting an eye on Josie who was wiggling all over as she chatted up the workmen. I cast another eye on Jamie who was butter-bright in conversation with the policemen; and I cast a third eye at Frances who was beaming moistly, and in love with the policeman who was patting her hand.

So everything was under control – though I didn't yet know why Frances had fainted.

I left the restaurant, wandered round the corner and found one policeman teetering beside the excavated pavement, Lenny bent double peering into a hole, and a man's grey head showing out of the hole, scratching itself as if it couldn't believe its eyes.

5

'Hello,' I said.

The policeman glanced at me. Lenny said, 'HE DOESN'T KNOW WHAT IT IS,' and the grey head in the hole shook, then nodded in agreement.

'Are you the police doctor?' I asked.

'Umph,' he sighed. 'Know anything about this? No, of course you don't. Why should you? Not a hoaxer are you? Not an osteopathic surgeon are you, trying to fool a poor police doctor? No, no. Ever seen the like? I ask you – ever seen the like?'

He talked on, but his hand gestured into the hole, so I crouched and saw the skeleton.

Its ribs curved out of the earth, one freshly broken; and as Jamie had said, the skeleton was narrow. Or was it Josie?

I saw the shine of a pelvis amid the dirt, and it too, was narrow; why, facing such a person on a dark night you'd mistake him for a gate post – if he was standing near a gate.

I was saving the face for last.

Not a face, of course. Just the bone-pale glimmer of cheeks, and a smile too full of teeth to be human.

The doctor bent, using a clean paintbrush to sweep soil from the forehead. He said, 'It keeps falling in.' Meaning the soil.

I said, 'Huh! Huh! Huh!' as horns appeared. 'Sheep,' I suggested. 'Look for a sheep with its horns cut off.' I nodded at the skull.

'I wish it were that simple,' groaned the doctor. He raised his elbow, and I helped him out of the hole.

'Cup of tea?' I offered.

We left the policeman persuading Lenny not to fall into the hole, and entered the restaurant.

The young policeman was back at his table, eating. Frances was hovering. Josie was still wiggling around the workmen. Common taste has my daughter.

The policemen made a space for the doctor, and I asked if he wanted lunch.

'Tea. You work here?'

'My place,' I smiled.

'Anybody dig up that pavement in the last few months? I mean to say, just how long *have* you been here?'

I moved to the counter to make his tea.

'All my life,' I said across the restaurant, 'running this place. Before that, I went to the village school. I don't remember the pavement being dug up. Milk on the table. Would you like a toastie?'

The doctor shook his head. The policemen were waiting for him to speak. So were the workmen at the other table. Josie pouted at being ignored, and stopped wiggling.

The doctor raised his cup to the workmen. 'You did well! Well – you did. Uncovered him beautifully. Just one rib snapped with a spade—'

'Shovel,' said a workman 'That was me. I found it. I found it, didn't I, lads?'

'He found it,' Josie assured us, and patted the man's shoulder.

The workman spoke to the doctor as if breaking a rib with his shovel qualified him in forensic science. 'Murder was it, and the horns stuck on after? Sick, some people are—'

Nods from his table.

'Now, now, now!' rumbled the doctor. 'I have no evidence of murder, so please don't start rumours, gentlemen. I have seen no broken bones – apart from his rib – to suggest violence. Of course, he could have been stabbed in the back—'

'Hit on the head?' demanded Jamie over a policeman's shoulder.

'Umph,' agreed the doctor. 'Once we get him out I can tell more. Considerable smell of mothballs in here.' The doctor's nose hovered around.

Then: 'Lady in a hurry,' he remarked, as someone bustled in. 'Deaf in her left ear,' commented the doctor. 'Heart strong. Arthritic—'

The lady hobbling into my restaurant was Mrs Patience of Rose Cottage.

She did not look pleased.

6

'Right,' said Mrs Patience, 'Who's in charge?'

Her glance burned across the workmen, condemned Josie for standing with a man, and made the police look guilty for eating instead of policing. One of the policemen was an inspector, and he drew a breath to reply, but Mrs Patience fastened her eye on to the doctor's grey hair and decided.

'You're in charge! What's your name? I like knowing who I'm talking too. Speak up.'

'I'm Doctor Alexander. But really—' He waved at the inspector.

'What have you found out?'

'Found out? Well—'

'Speak up!'

'WELL . . .'

'Have you – or have you not – found out what is haunting my cottage?'

'There's been subsidence, missus,' said a workman. 'Your pavement was sinking. We were digging—'

'I know *that!*' snapped the old lady. 'I reported it, didn't I? Right outside my front window!'

'Haunted, Mrs Patience?' I said.

'Eh?' she asked, turning her right ear to me.

'You didn't tell me you were haunted!' I said. 'If I'd known—'

'You?' she demanded. 'Why should I tell you? You don't listen! I told the police last Monday. But they don't take trouble with the living, do you?' she accused the policemen, '—but when somebody dead turns up, you appear, like flies on a cow pancake!'

Cackles from the workmen. Giggles from Josie. I saw a workman's hand round her waist. Thirteen, she is. I used my hardest glance on the workman, and his hand removed itself. For goodness' sake.

Thirteen. I hoped Josie wasn't going to be trouble. She has hair like Esther's, which flops around her face giving her a mysterious look. Maybe I mentioned that. Come to think of it, maybe it's Josie who brings in the men customers. I swept around for Frances, and found her behind the young policeman, open-mouthed at what Mrs Patience was saying. Maybe Josie was as attractive as Frances – even though she was only thirteen – because she was flirty. Oh.

I understood. I nodded to myself. Thirteen and a flirt. My Josie was just realising that men and girls were different, and her flirtiness was her trying out her powers.

So that was all right.

Then everybody stood up.

My restaurant was suddenly heaving with blue uniforms and workmen's strong bodies all milling for the exit with Jamie and Mrs Patience in the lead.

Josie and Frances were left gaping like stranded fish.

'Can I go too, Dad?' whispered Josie.

'Go? Where are they going? They haven't paid!' I raised my voice. 'Gentlemen!'

But they flowed out of the restaurant without looking back.

'May I go?' demanded Josie.

'Where?' I asked.

'Rose Cottage! Don't tell me you weren't listening!' She ran after Jamie.

'Frances,' I commanded, 'stay where you are.'

Esther bumped from the kitchen and gazed at the empty tables.

'Rose Cottage,' I said, and followed my children towards adventure.

7

That's how I felt. Towards adventure.

The policemen and workmen (with Lenny looming among them), gazed down into the hole in the pavement where the skeleton lay, as they waited for Mrs Patience to open the front door of Rose Cottage.

They filed into the cottage, leaving the dug-up pavement to the policeman on guard, treading earthy footprints on to the doorstep.

I trod my earthy footprints on to the doorstep too. I'd never been in Rose Cottage. It smelled of tea and hoovered carpets and the fresh air that accompanied us visitors.

We shuffled to a halt.

I noticed that Lenny wasn't with us.

Usually he is as curious as a kitten; then I recalled him shuffling off down the street, looking as if the crowd was too much for him.

Then Josie's giggles arose out of the crush of bodies in the little hall. I squeezed in until I could shut the front door, which made the hall immediately gloomy.

'Down here, the lot of you!' I heard Mrs Patience's voice.

The crush slackened. Heads in front of me descended somewhere.

'Isn't it spooky?' whispered Jamie.

I didn't think it was spooky.

I was last to step down a staircase. When my feet reached the floor, my head was still upstairs in the hall.

I bent, and found myself in a cellar, with the policemen also bent, and the workmen squatting, because the ceiling was squashing us down. A bulb in the ceiling threw shadows from each man, shadows which clung to the stone walls like dark, flat people.

Josie's giggles soared, but cut off as Mrs Patience snapped, 'Mind your ankles on the lawnmower! Don't sit on that box!' A workman leapt before his bottom descended on to a long cardboard box which – from the printing on it – had once held the lawnmower. 'Now listen.'

We listened.

Backs creaked as policemen hesitated between standing with their shoulders against the ceiling, or crouching. The workmen seemed comfortable in any position, one sitting against the lawnmower and patting his lap in invitation to Josie.

I said, 'MY DAUGHTER IS ONLY THIRTEEN,' and the workman blushed. Josie sighed, 'Da-ad,' amid chuckles.

'Hush!' from Mrs Patience, and she leaned towards the doctor and glared at him.

'Quiet now,' said the doctor.

I wondered why we were being quiet. Mrs Patience had said in the restaurant that her cottage was haunted. I had heard *that*. But I'd missed what she'd said next; probably mentioned the symptoms of the haunting.

Anyway, here we are in the cellar, I told myself, with the dug-up pavement – I realised – just through the cellar's stone wall, though level with the ceiling.

A car rumbled past. I glanced behind me to see where we had come down the little staircase, and, as I looked, the door at the bottom of the staircase moved.

For a moment, I thought Frances had followed us, despite being told to stay in the restaurant. But I knew she wouldn't leave Esther on her own. Then I thought maybe the policeman on guard had stepped into the cottage and was having a little joke. I thought Ha! Ha! and was shushed by Mrs Patience; I hadn't meant to laugh out loud: Then I remembered that no one could have followed me in, because I'd shut the outside door.

You do appreciate that all this thinking only took a second. When I'd finished thinking, and Mrs Patience had shushed me, the cellar door was slowly swinging away from me, closing.

Then I knew why.

I had heard a car passing.

'Ho! Ho! Ho—!'

'Will you be quiet, Allan Henderson!' shrieked Mrs Patience.

So I was quiet; but I smiled as the door closed completely, because – of course – the vibration of the car had caused the door to shut. Either that, or somebody passing through the hall had slipped down the staircase and shut it. Which was silly.

I shook my head more, and caught Jamie's frown. I smiled; and he sighed and looked away.

This was something he'd kid me about later, telling me I was laughing like some thicko – but he'd know all right that his Dad was on the ball, spotting something nobody else had spotted. 'Ha! Ha!' I thought and 'Shut ups' muttered around me.

Then I noticed something else.

Everyone was suddenly still. Even Josie was frozen, her head tilted, hair over one eye; staring at nothing.

Her eye blinked.

Jamie flickered a glance at me. Doctor Alexander had raised one hand as if about to grasp something; and around us, the shadows clung to the walls like painted people.

Then I heard.

Quite clearly, I heard.

8

I heard laughter.

I *had* wondered how Mrs Patience managed to hear any slight noise haunting her cottage, her being deaf in one ear, but you couldn't miss this if you were deaf in both ears with a bag over your head; and nobody – I can tell you – shushed whoever owned that voice.

The doctor's cheek paled.

Josie drew in a gasp, and Jamie's eyes met mine, pleading. But I couldn't get to him for bodies, and I saw his fist tighten as he crouched closer to the cellar floor.

I won't describe the voice that laughed.

I can't.

Silly words come to mind, like 'blood-curdling'.

From the shocked faces around me – and remember these were police and workmen – I knew that every one of us had felt our blood curdle.

And 'hair-raising'.

The doctor's hand moved to his head and pressed down the hairs on the back of his neck.

Josie sank on to the lap of the workman who was sitting against the lawnmower, but he seemed not to notice; and she curled against him – not like a flirt, but like a frightened little girl.

Then I remembered that the cellar door had shut. Silently.

I turned. The door seemed very shut indeed.

I didn't panic.

I run a busy restaurant. If I was the panicking type I would panic every day at the things that might go wrong in my kitchen.

I turned away from the door. The faces of the men around me reminded me of the faces of actors in a war film when bombs are dropping and there is nowhere to run.

That laughter cackled again through the cellar.

Josie leapt from the workman's lap and pushed through the crowd desperately. She clung to me. Jamie followed her, tears in his eyes, and I held him.

'It's not in here,' whispered the doctor.

He looked around for agreement. 'It's not here, inside the cellar?'

A nod from men near the front wall of the cottage.

'Outside that wall,' breathed a workman.

'Right.'

'He's right.'

'Aye.'

'You sure?'

'Sure!'

'Where we were digging.'

'The doctor's right—'

'Shush!' from Mrs Patience.

You could have heard a pin drop on to a cushion.

My children's fingers bit into me, but I didn't

complain. I would have taken them home; I could have, I was nearest the door. But the door had shut itself. I was even more scared of the door not opening.

Then we heard a different sound.

Heads tilted to listen.

Rain? Was it raining? The weather hadn't promised rain.

The police inspector turned up his palm as if to test for rain descending though the cottage, and a workman said, 'Earth!' in an eerie whisper, and his mates nodded.

'Earth?' said the doctor.

'Trickling. Eh?'

'Aye.'

'Right.'

'Earth. Sounds like rain, but it isn't. Trickling earth. That's what it is—'

'Hush!' I said, and they raised their eyebrows.

The sound of trickling earth was – like the laughter – outside the front wall of the house; and we began to move, partly to loosen our tense bent bodies, but partly because you can only be scared of a noise for a certain time, then you start thinking.

'It's somebody outside,' said a workman firmly. He addressed the inspector. 'Has that bobby guarding the hole got a sense of humour? Good at horrible voices, is he?'

'We couldn't hear him through the wall!' asserted the inspector palely.

'Sure we could. There's a vent to the outside.' He nodded, and we peered through the shadows and I saw a metal grid in the wall, immediately below the ceiling.

'Haunted,' I said, as if it was a joke; as if Josie and Jamie weren't clinging to me in fear; as if the doctor's cheek hadn't turned white. Everybody relaxed.

'Come on, you two,' I said.

Josie and Jamie unpeeled themselves from me. I took them to the door.

The door opened with a pull.

'I smell mothballs,' said Josie as cooler air fell on to us from the hall.

Up the stairs and into the hall we went, with a grumble of deep voices behind us, and Mrs Patience's, 'Get along! Get along!'

I opened the front door of Rose Cottage.

The policeman on guard at the hole stood straight and flicked away his cigarette.

He didn't seem – to me – as if he'd been laughing.

I stepped on to the road with my children, shuffling round the hole to let the men out of the cottage behind me.

Out they came.

Crowding the pavement.

The policeman on guard stared dutifully at nothing.

The inspector stopped, and looked into the hole.

The doctor's glance touched the inspector's face, then he too looked into the hole.

We all looked into the hole, except for the policeman on guard who still gazed at nothing.

Then he, too, looked into the hole.
He said, 'Oh–!'

9

I won't mention what he said.

Out of the workmen's mouths burst worse expressions.

The inspector was too busy turning from white to red, then back to white, to say anything.

I couldn't blame him, because the skeleton had gone.

That's right, no longer there.

Earth had trickled in around the hole. We had heard it trickling while we were in the cellar, the doctor thinking it was rain.

It was still trickling. The policeman's cigarette slid with the earth.

It slid down towards the bottom of the hole. The inspector was now expressing himself clearly to the flabbergasted policeman, but I tried not to listen as I watched the cigarette.

Smoke still trailed from its hot end. Dust gathered on its damp end. I pointed at the cigarette – really to take Josie and Jamie's attention from police language – but the kids stared just as I stared. Then the language ceased, and heads crowded round, peering into the earthy hole, as the cigarette reached the bottom.

Where it should have stopped.

It should have lain at the bottom of the hole and allowed the earth to cover it.

But it didn't.

It sank through the earth, and disappeared.

'Grab a shovel!' yelped Jamie, and he grabbed a shovel, but a workman wrested it from him, and jumped into the hole. He dug down, and threw earth up on to the inspector's shoes.

Quick thinking on my Jamie's part: if the cigarette had sunk, then so had the skeleton.

'Watch out,' warned another workman, as the earth trickled faster.

'Where's it all going?'

'It must be an old mine shaft!' yelled Jamie.

'Never been mines around here.'

Then the policeman who'd been guarding the hole redeemed himself. You know what I mean. He'd let the skeleton escape, now he made up for his error.

This is what happened.

The workman shovelled.

The more he shovelled, the more earth fell on to his boots. He lifted one boot high, but went on digging. He lifted the other boot. Earth fairly rushed down around his ankles. He swayed.

'I'm stuck!' he gasped. 'Here! I'm sinkin'!' His arms waved to keep his balance.

Suddenly he slid in up to his chest.

A cry of horror arose from us all.

The policeman dropped flat on to the edge of the hole and caught the man's wrist.

The workman's shovel nose-dived past his chest and vanished. The workman would have vanished too, if the policeman hadn't hung on to him. Many hands hoisted the man out of the hole, standing him on the road.

He whispered, 'There was nothin' under my feet! There was nothin' under my feet!'

Then he sat, gasping and white, and I didn't blame him, for down in that hole somewhere, was the owner of the voice that had laughed.

Then I saw that Josie was crying, and Jamie's lip was quivering.

'Gentlemen,' I said, and they all looked at me, including the man who had sunk. 'My children have had enough. I trust you will pay for your meals when convenient.'

Every face looked guilty. I knew they had simply forgotten. 'When you're ready,' I assured them, and I took Josie by the hand, and Jamie, and walked them back to the restaurant.

*   *   *

'Frances.' The restaurant was quiet.

I sat Frances at a table.

I had some serious listening to do.

Frances fiddled with her wooden-smooth hair.

'I want to know,' I said sternly, 'why you fainted.'

Frances gazed at me in surprise, but I wasn't being stern with *her* – I was being stern with myself.

'I'm waiting,' I said, and her fingers released her hair.

'But I told you!' she cried.

'You know I don't listen,' I said. 'My mind wanders. Now tell me again.'

'Oh, Allan . . .! Oh. Oh, even if you are listening, you won't believe me, but the woman in the wheelchair had a forked tongue! There. I said you wouldn't believe me! I should've kept it to myself—'

But I did believe her.

I wasn't even surprised. People who made my hair stand on end ought to have forked tongues.

'Frances,' I said, 'get yourself a cup of tea. Have a free cake.'

I left her blinking, and found Esther in the kitchen feeding Josie and Jamie who had forgotten their tears after their shock in Rose Cottage.

I looked hard at my wife.

I said, 'Esther, I know why Frances fainted, and she may be ready to tell you. It's not pleasant, but I think it's important. I'm going now, to make sure that Mrs Patience is all right. I don't think any of the policemen stayed with her.'

I left Esther and my children gaping at me over their late-lunch pizzas: I'm not usually firm.

The police had gone from outside Rose Cottage – except for the constable guarding the hole.

'What are you up to?' he demanded, hardly raising his eyes from the earth which had stopped trickling.

'Visiting a friend,' I said, knocking on Mrs Patience's door.

I knocked again, and waited to hear Mrs Patience grumbling through her hall, but I heard only silence.

'Did she go out?'

'Nobody gets past me,' shrugged the constable toughly.

'Except skeletons,' I said.

I strolled round the side of the cottage and into the back garden.

The kitchen door was ajar.

Maybe Mrs Patience usually left it open.

I approached, and a doormat inside waited for my feet.

I let it wait.

'Mrs Patience?'

I remembered she was deaf.

'MRS PATIENCE.'

I pushed the door, and stepped on to the mat.

Every cupboard in the kitchen was open.

'Mrs Patience!'

I went through the kitchen to the hall, and peeped into a bedroom.

The bedcovers had been lifted at the corners, as if someone had looked under the bed. A suitcase lay empty on the carpet. And the wardrobe was open.

In the sitting-room, the sideboard doors gaped, showing the inside full of dishes.

Somebody, I told myself, had been searching for something; and Mrs Patience wasn't answering her name. And the policeman hadn't seen her go out, and I hadn't passed her in the back garden.

'Therefore,' I told a cigar box on the sideboard, 'in the few minutes since I was here with the police and the workmen, Mrs Patience has disappeared.'

I remembered that I hadn't looked in the cellar.

The cellar steps invited me down.

I accepted their invitation nervously, then pushed open the door, and darkness sparkled as darkness does when you stare into it.

I found the light switch, and shadows rose in every corner.

I stood bent under the ceiling.

I could smell mothballs again, and I noticed a

pile of clothes beside the outer stone wall.

'Mrs Patience?' I said – not that she'd be lurking in the dark, but . . .

You know.

A tallboy stood with its back to a shadow.

I approached, and felt around in the shadow but Mrs Patience wasn't there.

I said, 'Hum,' and straightened, and observed that the drawers of the tallboy drooped open, with gatherings of mothballs inside.

I guessed that someone had taken the clothes from the drawers and piled them beside the wall.

Though I couldn't think why.

Then I noticed that part of the wall, near the clothes, had no cement between the stones – as if someone had picked the cement out.

Not that it mattered.

Next, I opened the cardboard box that the workman had almost sat on, but it was full of newspapers.

The way the old lady had shrieked, you'd've

thought her wedding china was in it.

I lifted some of the papers, noticing they were dated 1963. And that didn't matter either. I was worried about Mrs Patience. I anxiously hauled out more papers.

I know what you're thinking. The same as I was thinking. That Mrs Patience was inside, all murdered and folded to fit into the corners of the box.

Well, she wasn't.

Under the papers was a gigantic glass jar.

And in the jar was a dead child.

I leaned closer.

Perhaps it wasn't a child. A hairless monkey, maybe, squashed in tight, preserved in clear liquid.

Then I saw horns pointing from the skull.

Then I saw a forked tongue dangling from the lips.

Then the eyes opened.

And they looked at me.

10

How I left the cellar calmly, I'll never know. I suppose we all have strengths we don't normally use.

I met Mrs Patience coming in the back door, and we stared at each other.

I think she knew that I had seen the devil in the jar.

She waved me back into the kitchen.

I sat on a stool while she filled the kettle.

She closed all the open cupboards and gave me a curious look.

I shook my head. She knew I wouldn't search her cupboards.

'There's nobody here,' I said, as she moved as if to peer into the hall. 'I don't think anything's been stolen.'

She made tea. She rummaged until she found a biscuit tin.

We sipped the tea and nibbled the biscuits.

I was on my third biscuit before she said, 'You saw it?'

I nodded.

She said hopefully, 'I thought it might be gone.' She laughed with less humour than yesterday's milk. 'It's been there since 1963,' she sighed. 'I thought it might have dissolved.'

Her eyes wandered guiltily.

'Huh! Huh!' she laughed. 'Is it dead?'

'No.'

Sip. 'Fancy.'

'Mrs Patience—'

'Aye, aye, aye!' she snarled. 'Give me time! D'you think it's something a body can just come out with?'

I let her scowl into her tea.

'My neighbour gave me tea. Just now. That's where I've been. It was my fault for nagging.'

I wondered why she'd nagged her neighbour for

tea – but she wasn't talking about the tea.

'I nagged for new clothes,' said Mrs Patience. 'And new shoes. I liked shoes when I was younger. But it was Jimmy's fault as well.

'He was a fool buying that book! He worked on the railways. Not that *that's* got anything to do with it, but it shows how ordinary he was. An ordinary big man working on the railways, buying a book like *that!* He could do card tricks, you see, and wee bits of magic. So he thought he was qualified to use this book. I'll show it to you later. I told him, "Why don't you magic me some new clothes instead of wasting money on something you can't read!"

'And he couldn't read it, for it was in Latin.

'But you had to admire him because he went to night classes and learned Latin. I suppose I was surprised. Though why he bothered . . . The sight of the book put me off, with its horrid title and horrider pictures! Ugh!'

The old lady shivered.

'Then he conjured up a devil – you saw it in the

jar, Allan. Jimmy said I could have all the clothes I wanted now; and sure enough, the devil got me clothes.

'I was pleased, despite being anxious having a devil in the house. I had a figure in those days, and enjoyed showing myself off. I was only a railwayman's wife, but I fair surprised the neighbours with my outfits.

'Which was my mistake. People talked. How could Agnes Patience afford all these clothes and shoes? I had to lie – tell them a relative had left me a wee drop money.

'I hated lying. Then I discovered that the devil didn't conjure the clothes up innocently like a genie in a pantomime.

'It stole them.

'That was too much. I put the clothes away in the tallboy in the hall, and told Jimmy to get rid of that *thing!*

'But Jimmy's Latin wasn't good, and getting rid of the devil was on a different page of the book, and he couldn't tell which. So we were stuck with the beast.'

Mrs Patience set her teacup aside.

I asked, 'You put it in the jar?'

'Not right away. You see, it ate too much.

'It ate and ate and ate. Fortunately, it got its food the same way it got the clothes – by stealing! So feeding it didn't cost anything – though the village weans got blamed for food disappearing from shop counters. The devil could slip about, you understand, always just at the corner of your eye, so you thought it was a child playing behind you, or a bit of furniture . . .

'But it didn't *slip* about the house – oh, not it! It roamed from room to room, stuffing cakes into its mouth as if it had never eaten before, leaving crumbs everywhere, and it didn't like hoovering, so I had to do that. I got into the habit. I do it yet. I hoover every day because I don't feel the house is clean otherwise. And besides . . .'

Mrs Patience sat, her old face blank.

I leaned towards her. She was very still.

Had she died?

'Don't stare, Allan Henderson!'

'Sorry. You said, "besides". Besides what, Mrs Patience?'

'Oh, nothing. Nothing at all. Don't fuss! Give me a glass of water!'

'There's still tea in the pot,' I suggested, but she waved away the tea *and* the glass of water *and* the whole wide world!

I wondered what she had been about to tell me.

'We were going mad with worry,' she said. 'We couldn't have friends in. When the postman came we were sick in case he would catch sight of the devil wandering through the hall. Then, one Christmas Day, it stole Jimmy's bottle of gin.'

'A bottle of gin?'

'The brute drank the lot. You should have heard my Jimmy. Talk about bad language . . . !

'Then he calmed down, Jimmy did. But his eyes were like stone, as if he'd gone out and left his face behind. No expression, you understand. I'd never seen him so strange.

'That was on the Christmas Day. On the Boxing Day I saw a smile on his lips, oh! an odd wee smile which gave me hope, but at the same time made me scared. I wondered if he'd thought of a way of killing the devil, even though we knew *that* was impossible for it said so in the book. We'd thought about it often enough, I can tell you.'

I frowned. The skeleton under the pavement meant that one devil, at least, was dead.

But I listened to Mrs Patience.

'The day after Boxing Day, Jimmy brought home three crates of gin—'

'Three *crates*?'

'—which he hid. I started to demand why he'd spent so much on drink, when he put a finger on my mouth. I stopped talking, amazed at the look on his face.

'He glanced behind me, I remember, and smiled. And I looked around, but the devil wasn't there;

stuffing its face in the kitchen, no doubt.

'After that, I didn't mention the gin because I knew my Jimmy was planning something. Maybe he wasn't such a fool. Folk who can think up tricks can't be that silly.

'He was out first-thing the next morning and didn't come back till after the shops shut. I reckoned he'd been to the city. But he'd bought nothing. It was into January before he came home one day very late from work, all pleased, but tired, though still carrying nothing. Then a shop's van arrived, and men delivered the jar.

'They stood it in the hall. It was as high as my elbow, with a glass stopper the size of a soup-pot lid. The stopper had a red rubber washer around the underside to make a secure seal and a metal clamp on the top like a preserving jar, to prevent it popping out.

' "Help me," says Jimmy, once the shop men had left.

'So we shuffled the jar down the cellar steps,

Jimmy shushing me loudly not to let on – though I was saying nothing.

'I knew he wanted the devil to hear us and think the jar was a secret.

'So we put the jar in the cellar and fetched the gin and poured the gin into the jar, bottle after bottle. Three dozen of them – that's thirty-six if you can't count the old way. Even then, the jar was only a third full; and the smell perfumed the air of the cellar, the fumes setting us giggling. Then Jimmy made me take a mouthful from the last bottle and he took a mouthful too, before emptying that bottle into the jar. Then we sprawled on the earthy floor, breathing gin, pretending to sleep.

'I lay with my eyes almost shut and managed a snort, my hand among the empty bottles; and I saw the devil's brown little feet reaching down the cellar steps.

'Down it came, quietly – because it knew it wasn't allowed gin due to its drunken behaviour at Christmas. It stood beside us looking at the empty bottles, looking at me, looking at Jimmy who snored realistically. It looked at the jar one-third full of gin, then at the stopper on the floor, and oh, the fumes wafted wonderfully.

'Huh. My Jimmy wasn't such a fool, after all. The devil fell for his trick. The jar was almost as tall as it was, so the devil – its tongue flickering quick as a snake's – put its hands on the rim, pulled itself up and stuck its head inside.

'Jimmy opened his eyes wide. He crinkled his cheeks at me and up we leapt! We grabbed the devil by its legs and stuffed it headfirst into the jar. In an instant the stopper was in place and the metal clip sprung shut.

'Oh, what a commotion! What a struggling went on in that jar! But the brute had no room to move; and the gin now filled the jar right to the stopper because the devil took up most of the space.

'How it glared. How it glared and cried out in a bubbly voice. It didn't drown. We knew it wouldn't. Oh, I know! it seemed to breathe when it was wandering about our house, but being in the gin didn't trouble it. But it couldn't get out, and that was all we cared about.

'Then – while we were still high on fumes and triumph – in other words before we lost our nerve – we toppled the jar into the cardboard box and covered the devil with newspapers. Later – we told each other – we would dig up the cellar floor and bury the box and the jar with the devil inside it, six feet down.'

Mrs Patience looked at her hands as if she was expecting to see her glass of water.

'But we never did,' she sighed.

'Maybe we were scared. Maybe we didn't want to feel like murderers – though the beast would live on. Maybe we didn't want to do something as permanent as burying it alive. For all we knew it would stay buried for a thousand years, and we couldn't be that cruel.

'And we rather forgot, I suppose.

'You know – we put it out of our minds.

'We began – eventually – to use the cellar again, not thinking about the devil one bit. The tallboy was in the hall in those days, where I kept some of Jimmy's clothes, and the clothes the devil had brought me, because I couldn't afford to throw them out; even though I didn't dare wear them.

'Oh,' sighed Mrs Patience.

Then she wept while I made another pot of tea.

11

Mrs Patience stopped dabbing her eyes, and sipped her tea. I said, 'I don't understand . . .'

Her old face wrinkled into a smile.

I couldn't remember ever seeing her smile. She said, 'Thank you for listening, Allan. What were you going to say?'

I said, 'I don't understand why you risked taking the policemen and workmen into your cellar? You knew the devil was in the jar. Someone could have found it. And how could you go into the cellar again, knowing it was haunted by that terrible laughter?'

I wondered if I'd asked too many questions, but Mrs Patience talked on, though her voice trembled.

'But I hadn't heard the laughter before,' she wobbled. 'The cellar was haunted by other noises –

scrapings and scratchings that I wasn't sure I was hearing because I'm a wee bit deaf in this ear. It had been going on for days. I thought maybe it was folk walking past on the pavement which is level with the cellar ceiling—'

'I noticed that.'

'—but the noises got louder, as if something was burrowing closer. I was getting nervous, and needed help, so I asked the police to come, but they didn't. They know I'm just a crabbit old woman and not worth their time.

'Then the pavement subsided and the workmen came this morning, and found the skeleton. *Then* the police came. I'd nearly forgotten the devil in the jar.

'Not really, of course, but it had been in the cellar since 1963, and it was no more important now than the lawnmower. It was only when that workman went to sit on the box . . .'

She shook her head. 'Then while you were chortling to yourself like an idiot—'

I raised my eyebrows.

'—I thought I heard the digging again. And that's when I hushed everybody. Then we heard that laugh.

'You all got out fast enough and forgot about me. Though *you* came back, Allan. You're a good soul, even if you're not very bright. But I needed company – which is why I went next door . . .'

Mrs Patience passed me her cup and I offered her more tea, wondering if I should protest at being called not very bright. I considered myself brighter than most people. Just because I don't listen . . .

She was shaking her head, and I thought she was tired of me, but she was only refusing the tea. Anyway, I had another question to ask.

'Where did that skeleton come from, Mrs Patience?'

Her old eyes stared at me. Then she gazed out of the kitchen window, but she wasn't seeing the garden.

I said, 'It must have been there a long time.'

'Maybe.'

She knew something.

She gazed at nothing.

Then she whispered, 'It's devils who are digging, Allan. Undermining the pavement, making it subside. That's what I've been hearing in my cellar. It's not haunted. Unless you call devils digging, a haunting. A haunting.' Her voice rose into a thin song.

'A-haunting we will go, a-haunting we will go, eeh-oh my Daddy-oh, a-haunting we will go.'

'Have you had any lunch?' I asked quietly.

'I think so. Yes, my neighbour had some soup ready. Before the tea.'

'Do you want to lie down?'

'Aye.' She stood up, and I helped her to the bedroom.

I pushed the suitcase under the bed with my foot, and shut the wardrobe door.

'I'll rinse the cups,' I said, 'then leave you to rest.'

'Aye.'

So I rinsed the cups and the teapot. Then I
trotted round the rooms silently and shut all the
cupboards. I thought of going into the cellar and
covering the devil again with the newspapers, but I
didn't quite have the nerve. So I whispered,
'Cheerio,' and slipped out through the kitchen.

The policeman had gone, and the hole was
covered with old doors and surrounded by traffic
cones.

I wandered back to the restaurant, my head full
of weird images, the strangest being old Mrs
Patience – or young Mrs Patience as she was then –
and her husband toppling the devil into the jar of
gin. Why, I nearly laughed. And I remembered too,
that she hadn't been upset at someone searching
her cupboards. As if she had guessed who had done
it.

I found Esther idling behind the counter, with
Josie and Jamie wiping tables as slowly as possible,
and Frances sitting talking to a chap in a jumper

who looked familiar and was playing with her little finger.

'This is Brian,' blushed Frances, and I nodded at Brian, thinking how quickly Frances had fallen out of love with the young policeman.

'He's the policeman who rescued me after I fainted,' murmured Frances, glowing as pink as a flower. 'He's our new village bobby. He's just come off duty.'

'Oh,' I said, remembering that I had rescued Frances and sat her up at the table. 'Hello,' I said.

'Hello,' said Brian. 'How's the old lady? Frances mentioned you'd gone to the cottage.'

'She's lying down,' I told him. 'Upset, you know.'

'That laugh was something,' agreed Brian.

I hadn't realised Brian had been in the cellar too.

'Have you mentioned—' I stuck out my tongue at Frances who looked shocked for a moment.

'The forked tongue,' I explained.

'Oh. Yes,' she said. 'I told Esther.'

'Really strange,' agreed Brian.

'Yes. Excuse me.'

I retreated to the kitchen and sat on a stool. I wanted to think.

Esther bumped in beside me, and I said, 'Right, Esther,' and she said, 'I didn't speak, Allan,' and went out with a box of tea bags.

I thought again about Mrs Patience and her Jimmy heaving the devil into the jar.

I thought about Mrs Patience not worrying about her cupboards being searched.

But my memory kept pushing the tallboy into my mind. I could see this piece of furniture with its back in shadow in the cellar, and mothballs in its drooping drawers. Mrs Patience had said that she'd put the clothes the devil had stolen for her into the tallboy – though it was in the hall in those days.

I had already figured that the clothes piled beside the cellar wall had come out of the tallboy – but what did it mean?

What *could* it mean?

For a second my mind went blank.

Then things came together – and I sat up straight on the kitchen stool.

I smiled.

Not very bright, am I?

I jumped off the stool, and bumped through to the restaurant, taking Esther with me from behind the counter.

We interrupted Brian's finger-twiddling with Frances.

Josie and Jamie drifted close.

'Sit down,' I said.

They sat down.

I repeated Mrs Patience's story.

When I had finished, mouths stared at me.

'And there's more,' I informed them, 'that Mrs Patience didn't tell me.'

'So how do you know, Dad?' asked Jamie, 'if Mrs Patience didn't tell you?'

I smiled at my son.

'I worked it out.'

'Your father worked it out,' Esther assured our children.

'Thank you, Esther. The pavement,' I said, 'outside Rose Cottage, subsided—'

'This morning,' nodded Josie. 'That's why the workmen came. We know that, Dad.'

'It subsided,' I explained, 'because the devils were digging under it – digging their way out from deep inside the earth. They needed to get into Rose Cottage to rescue the devil they hadn't seen since before 1963—'

'The one in the jar!' sighed Brian.

'—though why they came up under the pavement instead of through the cellar floor . . .'

'They missed, Dad,' said Jamie.

'Maybe,' I said. 'However, they *were* under the pavement, which meant they had to break through the cellar wall to get into the house. Some of the stones of the wall,' I explained, 'had no cement between them. However – once they were through the wall, they built it up after them so the hole wasn't obvious.

'Then they found the clothes in the tallboy.

'My guess is,' I continued, 'that they also found money, because when they left the restaurant here, they paid for their pizzas and cakes. They did pay, didn't they, Esther?'

'I had to count it out for them,' whispered my wife.

'There you are then,' I said. 'And after eating forty-two cakes, they returned to the cottage to start searching. But Mrs Patience was there, so, naturally, they waited until she went out.

'She came here to the restaurant to ask the police why they hadn't investigated her haunted cellar.'

I smiled knowingly at my audience.

'Mrs Patience,' I told them, 'leaves her back door unlocked.'

'So the devils just walked in,' said Josie.

'That's right. But before they could find the devil in the jar, we followed Mrs Patience back to the cottage—'

'With the policemen!' said Jamie.

'And those workmen,' murmured Josie.

'—and we were no sooner in the cellar, when the devils closed the door on us so we wouldn't hear them opening cupboards. But before they could do much, that ghastly laugh made our hair stand on end, and we trooped out again.'

'I smelled mothballs!' cried Josie. 'Didn't I say, Dad, that I smelled mothballs when we came out?'

'Yes,' I said, 'you did.'

'Dad!' cried Jamie. 'The devil who laughed! Behind the wall! I know what he was doing! He was rescuing the skeleton! Sure he was, wasn't he?'

'Um, yes . . . Yes. That's what he was doing.' I hadn't thought of that. 'Well done, Jamie. So. We left. And Mrs Patience went through to her neighbour, leaving the devils free at last, to search the house.

'But five minutes later, I went back and found all the cupboards open, and a pile of mothbally clothes beside the cellar wall.'

I paused.

'I don't get it,' said Josie.

Brian shook his head.

'The devils were searching . . .' said Jamie thoughtfully, 'and heard you coming, Dad . . . So they ran down to the cellar . . .'

'Right. Where they took off . . . ?' I encouraged him.

'They took off . . .' said Jamie, '. . . the clothes. Oh, I get it! They took off the clothes, then went back through the cellar wall!'

'And built it up after them. Well done!'

Esther pressed my hand.

'Smug, Dad,' sighed Josie. 'Makes sense.'

I smiled as I sat back from the table.

A man deserves the respect of his family.

12

Rose Cottage lounged quietly behind the hole decorated with red and white traffic cones.

The front door stood sedately shut as if burnt toast was the worst thing that could trouble its occupant.

We knew better, Brian and I.

Brian was with me to see the devil in the jar. The devil was evidence, so that the police could do something about these visitors to our village.

I knocked on the door.

We waited.

We looked at the cones around the hole.

We heard the old lady's feet trailing through the hall.

'It's me, Mrs Patience. Allan Henderson.'

The door opened and Mrs Patience stared out. 'I was lying down.'

I nodded. I had seen her safely to her bedroom.

'I didn't undress,' she said. She led us into the sitting-room where I had last seen her sideboard doors agape.

'Who's this?'

'Brian. He's a policeman. I wanted him to see the . . . devil in the jar. Maybe he can do something about the haunting.'

'Sit down. Maybe he can. Maybe he can't.'

We sat down.

'I worked something out, Mrs Patience.'

I explained my idea about the devils searching her cupboards.

'Oh,' said Mrs Patience. 'I thought as much.'

I looked at Brian and he raised his eyebrows.

'What I told you earlier,' said Mrs Patience, 'was only part of the story. Where are my manners? Would you like a cup of tea?'

We shook our heads. 'Allan,' said Mrs Patience

sinking into a chair. 'Would you mind? The kettle . . . ?'

I nodded and went to the kitchen. I made tea and took it to Mrs Patience in the sitting-room.

She tasted it and her eyes glittered at me over her cup. 'Good tea,' she said deliberately, and I waited. She was up to something.

'Strong,' she said, her eyes still glittering. 'Like my Lenny.'

She looked down and drank, leaving silence in the sitting-room except for the little slurp of her lips.

'*Your* Lenny?' I asked. I thought of Lenny eating his five bacon rolls, his arms covering the table in my restaurant.

'Lenny the Loony?' said Brian. 'Sorry,' he whispered.

'Lenny the Loony,' agreed Mrs Patience.

'He's *your* Lenny?' I wasn't sure what she meant.

'He's my son,' said Mrs Patience.

'No,' I said. 'I never knew.'

'Nobody knew.' Mrs Patience raised her chin. 'Nobody guessed. He doesn't look old enough – for one thing – to be my child. A simple mind keeps you young. Though he wasn't always simple. He was a normal wee boy, except . . .'

The glitter died from the old lady's eyes.

'Except?' I said.

'He was incredibly brave. And he was physically strong. He took after his father in that respect. My Lenny – my wee Leonard – tried to save his Daddy's life, and lost his wits in the process, and I was ashamed.'

Mrs Patience pulled her mouth up, pretending to smile.

'I was ashamed,' she squeaked, 'because he'd lost his wits.

'I was so ashamed that I let folk think he had died in hospital. But he didn't die, Allan. He lived, and got better. Though not completely better. So he stayed in hospital until he was old enough to live in a council house by himself.'

Mrs Patience drank her tea.

'I loved him, you understand. I can't explain how I could be ashamed of him and love him, both at once. I suppose it's the same in your house—'

I frowned at her. What did she mean?

But she talked on while I wondered what could be the same in my house . . .

Brian was prodding me.

'. . . my Leonard,' Mrs Patience was saying while she sniffed up tears, 'went down into Hell.'

And her smile stretched itself painfully across her old face while Brian and I gaped.

'Fetch me that book,' snuffled Mrs Patience.

I shut my mouth and looked around at the sideboard.

The cigar box I'd noticed earlier was among the old lady's ornaments, but I couldn't see a book.

'In the cigar box,' said Mrs Patience.

'Oh.' I fetched the box, and offered it to her.

'Open it.'

The tiny brass clasp was stiff.

'It hasn't been touched since 1963,' sighed Mrs Patience.

The clasp lifted, and I raised the lid. Inside lay a leather-bound book.

I tipped the book on to my palm.

'Read the title.'

'Um . . .' The title occupied the whole of the front cover and the lettering was old and curly, and difficult to read.

'DEMONOLOGIE . . . ?'

'That's it.'

'NECROMANCIE . . .'

She nodded.

'. . . AND DIVERS BLACK ARTS . . .'

'Go on.'

'. . . BEWARE ALL WHO OPEN THIS BOOKE LEST YOUR HEART BE NOT TRUE . . . THESE SORCERIES, SPELLS, RHYMES, RUNES AND MISCELLANIES OF MAGIC ARE WRITTEN IN LATIN, SO THAT THE

IGNORANT AND UNEDUCATED SHALL NOT WREAK DANGER ON THEMSELVES OR ON OTHERS. What does it mean?' I asked.

'It means that only a fool would read it!'

Mrs Patience, I could see, was having a rough time.

I passed the book to Brian.

Brian opened the book and sat still. Then he passed it back to me with a nod at the pages.

Squiggles of ancient Latin filled one page, but facing the squiggles was a creature so fearsome that I stopped breathing.

I tried to laugh, for the creature – if you thought about it – was horror-movie stuff with spikes fanning around its head, like the spokes from a bicycle wheel; and the face was blank darkness except for one circular eye shining in the middle of its forehead. More spikes glittered on its shoulders, and its gigantic hands sprouted fingers as thick and black and knobbly as . . . as something familiar, but for a moment I couldn't think what.

Oh, yes. As thick and black and knobbly as bicycle tyres.

Spokes and tyres?

Mrs Patience was talking, so I didn't worry about spokes and tyres and I didn't attempt to unravel the Latin, though a word or two translated itself, telling me that the creature was Agjam, Lord of the Devils who would appear in the distant future and take the devils to the upper world.

Or some such rubbish.

I closed the book and found Mrs Patience staring at me.

'Sorry,' I said.

'Leonard,' said Mrs Patience – obviously repeating herself, 'was in this house while the devil was here. Oh, I know! I didn't mention it earlier. I didn't want you to find out about him. I nearly told you though . . .'

I remembered Mrs Patience had started to say something when we'd talked before, then changed her mind.

'I remember.'

'My little boy,' said Mrs Patience, 'grew out of nappies and into schoolboy shorts while the devil was here.'

'But didn't Lenny . . . Leonard talk about the devil to people?' asked Brian.

'He was brought up with it. He thought everybody had one, I suppose; and even if he did mention it, folk would think he was making up stories. And besides, he could keep a secret. Let me get on! I must tell you while I have the heart! What we did next,' cried Mrs Patience, 'was to conjure up *another* devil!'

Mrs Patience opened her old eyes wide, but she was looking at nothing in the room; she was seeing into her past.

'This time,' she said quietly, 'to keep control of the second devil, we sealed it in a magic circle. Oh, I know how silly that sounds, and I know that I felt silly scratching the circle on the cellar floor while Jimmy read his bad Latin out loud from that book,

90

and waved a wand he'd cut from a rowan tree behind our gooseberries. And all the washing he did beforehand. "Part of the ritual, Agnes," he assured me, and he made me wash his clothes, while he bathed and rinsed himself – such goings on!

'But he conjured up the second devil.

'We kept the first devil in its jar, hidden in the cardboard box so as not to let on to the second devil where the first one was. Tell them nothing, you understand, because they can't be trusted.

'You should have heard the second devil fume and splutter! Oh, what a rage it was in! to find itself trapped in the circle. I must say, the first devil was much nicer. And I was proud of my Jimmy. He paid no heed to its blustering. He talked through all its rage and ranting until the silly thing realised it wasn't getting anywhere, and it began to listen.

'Jimmy told it that it must take its friend back to Hell.

'That was all. You'd think it would be simple. The sensible thing to do.

'But I suppose devils are only human. How it argued. Its friend had the right to annoy people if it wanted. And what right had we to return it to Hell? We had no right to conjure up any devils, and no right to use the book for it belonged to somebody called John Dee; and just because he died in sixteen-hundred and something, that didn't mean the book was ours . . .

'It seemed the devil had the right to do wrong, but we didn't have the right to do right. If you understand. I must say that Jimmy was wonderful.

'He ploughed through all the devil's silliness, insisting it should take its friend away.

'And it seemed the devil wanted – really – to take its friend. But it was being contrary, just to annoy us. Which is what devils do, I suppose.

'Then Jimmy said that our devil wasn't annoying anybody; and if the second devil didn't take it away, they could both stay where they were until the house crumbled on top of them – for the second devil couldn't get out of the circle.

'That shut the silly thing up. And though it fumed, it eventually agreed.'

Mrs Patience sniffed gigantically.

I poured more tea, which she gulped. 'The problem,' she said, 'was getting the devil in the jar into the circle. We'd scratched the circle in the earthy floor, but if we spoiled it while moving the jar, the new devil would escape. And my silly fool of a husband hadn't thought of that.

'So he read this book—'

Mrs Patience tapped the book.

'—while the devil smirked.

'I popped upstairs to the kitchen to make Leonard a piece-and-jam, because he'd been alone while we were in the cellar. Then – when Leonard was eating his crust – Jimmy yelled.

'Did I say that Jimmy was big like Leonard is now? He was. But how he yelled.

'I fled down the stairs, and my first sight was the cellar wall all tumbled into the magic circle - so the circle was broken; and behind the wall - under the pavement outside the cottage – was a low wee cave you could scarcely crawl into! And in the floor of this cave was a black hole, and my Jimmy was in the hole, his arms on the earth trying to pull himself out while the devil slapped at his head! Oh! Oh!

'I screamed, and rushed at the devil and beat it about its wicked ears, but it laughed its awful laugh – and I am ashamed! You have both heard how they laugh! Though our devil had never laughed like that! But I am ashamed because I hurried in terror to hide my face in the shadows.

'Leonard – I discovered – had followed me into the cellar. He was used to seeing a devil around the house, remember, so when he saw a devil hitting his Daddy, he wasn't afraid to help. He was eight years old with not a scrap of fear in him.

'From somewhere he'd picked up a hammer. He ran into the cave, but just as he reached the hole, Jimmy let go the edge and grabbed the devil. The devil had nothing but the ground to hold on to, and it yelped as Jimmy began to drag it with him.

Jimmy – you see – was sacrificing himself to prevent Leonard getting caught.

'But he didn't save Leonard, because the wee lad was too quick.

'Even as Jimmy grabbed the devil, Leonard dented its skull so that the brute flopped dead on the floor of the cave. Oh, I was surprised that a devil could die! But I had more to think about! For Leonard caught his Daddy by the wrist and Jimmy let go the devil! Oh, but his Daddy was too heavy, and as Jimmy fell down the hole he took our son with him. And I stood, the devil sprawled before me, and the cries of my man and my boy fading into the impossible drop, down into the final Darkness!'

13

In the sitting-room of Rose Cottage, I sat, aghast.

But Mrs Patience hadn't finished her story.

She sniffled – the poor old thing – and I shook myself and poured more tea, but she waved it away, panting, 'Later! Later. I'm full of tea! I must tell you the rest while I have the courage!'

But she sat weeping until I took her hand in mine, and she closed her eyes and clung to my fingers.

Brian shuffled as if he'd rather be with Frances.

It was minutes before Mrs Patience could speak.

She said, 'Thank you, Allan. You're a good man. Like my man was good; and maybe still is.'

Brian frowned, and I certainly wondered if I had heard correctly, but before I could ask what Mrs Patience meant, she talked on.

'I never saw my Jimmy again, but, oh, Allan, he really might be alive somewhere down that hole! Don't stare so! I'm not a stupid old woman! I'm not a wishful-thinking old fool kidding myself that Jimmy might be alive! Allan – he really *could* be alive!

'Don't you see? He and Leonard fell down that hole – *and Leonard came back!*'

I gaped. Of course Leonard had come back!

He was Lenny the Loony!

He was in the village right now!

'But how?' I cried. 'How could he have come back?'

'I don't know,' whimpered Mrs Patience. 'But I'll tell you what I do know. Oh dear. Maybe I *ought* to drink some tea.' Her head drooped.

I lifted her cup to her lips and she sipped, then glared, declaring that she could still lift a cup, thank you very much! Then she gulped and sighed until the cup rested empty in her palm.

She said, 'When Jimmy fell into that hole

dragging Leonard after him, I screamed. I screamed until my throat swelled and I could scream no more. Not a soul heard me. The village was quieter in those days, and nobody would pass my door for hours at a time.

'Eventually, I got a torch, and shone it down the hole. I would have given my life for my Leonard – now, when it was too late. At that moment, things dawned on me. First, that I didn't want anybody to know what had happened because nobody would believe me.

'And secondly, that I might find a way to get Jimmy and Leonard back – though how that could be, I had no idea. Oh, I was mad to think any such thing! Of course, I was! Wouldn't you be mad? Wouldn't you grasp at any straw?

'Then I thought of the devil still in the jar, and wondered if I could use it: swop it for Jimmy and Leonard if they were alive. Huh. Grasping at straws indeed. How could they be alive after falling down to the centre of the earth?

'I lay in the cave beside the body of the dead devil, and shone the torch down the hole. But all I could see were the rough sides and darkness. I had a crazy notion that I might climb down, because a strong person might find places to grip with their toes and fingers. But I was no climber. Just desperate. I tied string to the torch, a big ball of string; and I lowered the torch into the hole; and the torch spun slowly, a moving spotlight on the rocky sides. And down I lowered it, and the light spun and shrank with the distance; and more and more string slipped out between my fingers; the whole big ball, Allan! Down and down went the light, spinning slowly, as tiny as a spark in the chimney.

'Then the string ran out.

'Can you imagine my despair? My husband and my baby boy had fallen all that long and dreadful drop. I held the end of the string at arm's length and screamed their names over and over, but my voice was trapped in my swollen throat and their names tumbled hoarsely, fading, scarcely echoing at all, until the darkness beyond the prick of torch light, swallowed them up.

'I had meant to tie the end of the string to something to secure it until I could fetch another ball, and thus lower the torch twice as far. And I began to do this – I intended tying the string to the dead arm of the devil beside me. I didn't care about the devil. Not now. I had no fear now. But I could still be startled.

'And I was startled. I had pulled the end of the string out of the hole, but as I looped it around the devil's wrist, I jerked its arm, which moved the brute's head, so that its eyes looked at me, and I gasped, and let go the string.

'It whipped away into the hole. The devil, of course, was still dead and wasn't looking at anything. But the string was lost, along with the torch. I flung myself flat and stared after it.

'The torch glimmered like a single star which you can only see out the corner of your eye. Then it was gone.

'I listened. I lay with my head over the edge of that hole, and listened. I listened with my left ear for it seemed my left ear was my sensitive ear. I listened and listened, oh until my ear was numb with listening! Surely some sound must come up to me!

'But I listened, with the devil looking at me, and dark, black silence in my ear until I fell asleep.

'And, when I woke, the devil's gaze had turned white, and I felt unbalanced when I stood up.

'Then I realised that I was deaf in my left ear, and this was what was unbalancing me.

'I didn't know what to do. I knew that no one could help me. And I was in such distress! But despite my distress I could still be practical. Leonard would be missed at school, and Jimmy would be missed from his work on the railway.

'Then I thought of a plan.'

14

'I wrote a note to the school saying that Leonard was off-colour, and I was keeping him at home for a few days. I phoned the railway and told them that Jimmy's back was bad, and he couldn't get out of bed. It was as simple as that.

'Later . . .

'Time passed, you understand. I managed to pretend to neighbours that everything was normal; and, of course, I avoided them like I used to when the devil was in the house.

'Then I let on that wee Leonard had gone into hospital and we weren't sure what was wrong.

'Later I told the police that Jimmy had disappeared. This was a while after he'd fallen down the hole – when I was strong enough to tell lies to the police.

'Terrible things, lies. Then . . . Oh! Weeks afterwards! Oh, Allan, can I ever forget? You think I'm a crabbit old woman for no reason! But never has a mother suffered what I have suffered! No more tea! Let me tell you.

'I had wakened in the night in our big bed, lying on my back, my hand on the empty place beside me, my heart in the empty wee bed next door. Tears ran out of my eyes until I had to sit up and dry my ears with the corner of the sheet. And I thought I heard a noise.

'I stopped drying my ears and bent my right ear – my good ear – to the bedroom door, and I tell you, a chill swept up my back like a breath of north wind. Oh, Allan, the hairs on my arms rose as if I'd had an electric shock, for it seemed that I heard a child's voice.

'I heard my Leonard.

'It was true, Allan. I heard my Leonard, though I didn't believe it.

'I didn't believe it as I pushed back the bed

covers, and I didn't believe it as I crept into the hall.

'I simply couldn't believe such a thing as I listened at the cellar door, but the voice rang distantly, Allan, like an owl's screech across a moonlit field.

'And still I couldn't believe it. It must be my deaf ear ringing, I told myself, but I opened the cellar door and switched on the light. And I saw nothing in the cellar except the stones fallen from the wall, and the cave beyond and the devil all shrivelled and bony beside the black mouth of the hole, and I heard, I heard! my boy's blessed sweet voice crying, "Mummy!" but I couldn't step forward for fear I was dreaming and I'd wake up! Then—

'Out of the hole reached a little arm. Out of the hole reached another little arm, and Leonard's face popped up, and, "Mum!" he cried, and he slipped back, and I screamed and threw myself at him, and I landed up to my waist in the hole and caught his wrist as he dropped, and I pulled him up screaming, both screaming; screaming and screaming, shrieking and howling, hugging until we squeezed each other nearly senseless.

'How long we stayed mad down in the cellar, I can't tell.

'I took my Leonard into the kitchen. I don't think I asked him a single question; not even about his dad. And he stared at me as if he couldn't believe he was with me.

'And he stared at the kitchen, and he stared out into the hall and touched everything within reach as if he couldn't believe it was real. And I stared at him as if I couldn't believe he was real.

'I fed him. Bacon in a roll. Tea. More bacon in a roll. Huh, more tea. How he ate. I carried him through to my bed. I wrapped him up tight in my bed covers so that I wouldn't lose him again. I went into the hall. The cellar door had no lock. I wanted to be certain that Leonard couldn't get into the cellar.

'I pulled the tallboy from its place in the hall

and pushed it down the steps as if it weighed no more than a morning's shopping. It blocked the little staircase completely.

'Then I went into my bedroom and sat with Leonard through the night, never taking my eyes from him.

'My Leonard was safe.

'He was safe – but he wasn't well.

'He grew feverish. I called the doctor – not Dr Alexander in those days. The doctor said he had heard that Lenny was in hospital, though he had doubted how that could be without him knowing. I didn't say anything. It was obvious that Leonard was not in hospital but here in my bed. It was the doctor who started calling my wee boy 'Lenny'.

'Then Lenny really did go into hospital. And I visited him and visited him.'

Mrs Patience sighed sorrowfully.

'I loved him. I still love him. But he grew away from me. Whatever happened in the hole had taken his senses. One thing I did do, I remember, was shift the tallboy from the cellar staircase.

'I couldn't pull it up because it weighed a ton. How I moved it the night Lenny returned, with its drawers full, I'll never know. I certainly couldn't pull it back up the stairs.

'So I pushed it down. Fortunately, the cellar door opens inwards into the cellar. The tallboy is still there, as you know. I left the clothes in it. Oh, yes.

'Yes. And I filled in the cave with the earth Jimmy must have dug out the day he fell down the hole, and I rebuilt the cellar wall myself. I left the dead devil where it was behind the wall – beside the hole, you understand – where the workmen found its skeleton this morning.

'I realised – as I pushed the last stone into the wall – that the devils could be killed. I had hardly thought about that. The book had said they couldn't be killed, and we had believed it. Maybe whoever wrote the book had never tried hitting one with a hammer.

'It all happened,' sighed the old lady, 'a long time ago.'

Mrs Patience was exhausted.

I said, 'Should I send Esther round? To help you back to bed?'

But the old lady said she would make herself a meal first, and asked me to call again in the morning.

I left, remembering to take Brian with me – who had become as still as a piece of furniture while listening to Mrs Patience's terrifying story; and we forgot to look at the devil in the jar.

We avoided the old doors and traffic cones which kept people from falling down to Hell. I paused, staring at the doors. Or – I thought – to keep devils from popping up.

I hoped that old doors and traffic cones would be enough.

Brian went his own way, and I returned to the restaurant, and slept that night like a dead man.

* * *

Two blue uniforms walked among my restaurant tables next morning.

One uniform contained Brian who sighed at Frances, but didn't smile; the other contained the police inspector who frowned at Brian. They sat at a corner table glancing around to make sure customers couldn't overhear them, and asked me to join them for a cuppa.

We weren't busy that early, so I said, 'Certainly.'

Besides, the inspector's voice told me that his invitation should not be refused. I bumped through to the kitchen to ask Esther to take charge, and to change my apron for my jacket.

Josie and Jamie humphed at me because I had refused to tell them Mrs Patience's story; well, some stories are told in confidence, and Lenny being Mrs Patience's son seemed confidential to me.

I needn't have bothered keeping it secret.

As I bumped out of the kitchen to join Brian and the inspector, Mrs Patience marched into the restaurant, urging Lenny to follow her.

He stopped at the cake counter, swaying like an elephant.

Mrs Patience looked at the two policemen. She stared at my customers and saw they were locals. She steadied her glance on me and tried out a smile.

I knew what she was going to do.

With Lenny at her back, I knew.

I nodded, and Mrs Patience drew in a breath.

I said, 'I'll fetch Esther,' and Mrs Patience breathed out.

I called Esther from the kitchen. Josie and Jamie followed, and we waited awkwardly.

Mrs Patience took another breath—

'Morning!' cried a voice, and in swept Dr Alexander. 'Morning, everyone!' he announced. 'Morning, Inspector! Morning, Constable. Tea, Landlord! Ah, the lady who is deaf in her left ear! I beg your pardon. It's Mrs Patience from Rose Cottage. How's your arthritis?'

'I don't have arthritis!'

'I'm sorry. I thought you were hirpling the other day. I thought—'

'Hoovering!' shrilled Mrs Patience. 'It puts a strain on old hip bones. You said good morning to everybody except my son.'

'Your son?'

'Is there something wrong with my son, that you don't want to say good morning to him?'

Dr Alexander's mouth searched for words, and his eyes searched for Mrs Patience's son. He looked up at Lenny.

'My son,' declared Mrs Patience. 'That's what I came here to say. I've kept it a secret too long. Some of you will remember that my husband and I once had a little boy. You thought that he died in hospital. This is him. This is my Leonard, and I love him. He's the way he is, because . . .'

'Mrs Patience,' I said, 'people understand. Tea. Lenny . . . Leonard, sit here with your mother . . .'

Mrs Patience stood very straight.

'. . . beside the policemen.'

Dr Alexander joined them, and I sighed, and everyone sighed and returned to their cups and conversation, and Esther beamed at me with tears in her eyes, and I said, 'What?' but she just beamed more, and waved at Frances to stop gawping, and led Josie and Jamie into the kitchen.

'Well now,' said the inspector as I pulled a chair to the table.

We waited, and the inspector frowned, but said nothing.

Brian said, 'Um,' which I thought was almost as interesting.

Then Brian leaned anxiously towards Mrs Patience. 'I didn't see the devil in the jar yesterday, Mrs Patience, but since Allan told me about it, and your story confirmed it, I really had to tell . . .' He nodded towards the inspector.

'Did you?' said Mrs Patience, and took Leonard's hand.

'I didn't think a crime had been committed,' apologised Brian. He looked up at Frances. 'But if

I hadn't reported it, and something had happened later . . .'

'I understand,' said Mrs Patience with unusual kindness. Then I noticed that Brian was young enough to be her grandson.

Then she said, 'You tell them, Allan. You did listen, last night?'

I assured her that I had listened, and I told them; and when I had finished, Leonard said nothing, though it seemed that a smile stood at the corners of his lips. Then something rumbled, like a volcano under the table, or perhaps an earthquake rippling through the village – and Mrs Patience stood up in alarm – but it was only Dr Alexander gathering his voice for a remark.

He said, 'I've never seen a devil.'

Then he got to his feet, leaned both hands on the table, and raised his eyebrows.

15

The visit with Dr Alexander and the inspector to Rose Cottage felt like the end of the adventure for me.

The inspector would decide what to do about the hole.

And the doctor would no doubt take the devil-in-the-jar away and investigate the poor thing thoroughly.

Oh, well.

I had a restaurant to run.

So I ran it.

And Mrs Patience, I heard, moved out of Rose Cottage into the council house with her son.

This was just until the problem of the hole was solved, then she and Lenny would move into Rose Cottage permanently.

But the problem didn't get solved.

The workmen filled in the hole in the pavement. Dust from this work dulled the windows of Rose Cottage. Weeks later, when the filled-in earth had settled and the wind blew cold enough to bite your neck, the workmen paved the pavement so that you couldn't tell for sure where the hole had been.

And Rose Cottage seemed to sag.

Oh, it didn't really sag, but it looked tired and unloved. Ornaments disappeared from the inside windowsills and no doubt stood around prettily in Leonard's council house – though I never saw inside the council house.

And Mrs Patience was happy; Leonard's voice boomed less loudly. He and his mother popped into the restaurant for bacon rolls and pots of tea.

Then one day, a woman staggered into the restaurant with the knees of her tights burst, and blood running down her shins.

'I tripped on a paving stone. Outside that empty cottage.'

Esther took charge until the woman was fit to leave.

Not much of a story.

But shortly after that, a local family swarmed in around the fire shaking sleet from their clothes, the children worrying about their Labrador tied up outside.

Then: 'It did,' said the little girl earnestly to her mother.

The little boy nodded as if he wanted his head to fall on to his cake.

'Mutton barked like anything!' said the little girl. 'But it followed us across the field—'

'Footprints!' said her brother.

'Yes, it left lots of footprints in the sleet. And it shivered terribly, and fell over a lot—'

'Faceprints!' said the little boy seriously, and his mother caught my eye, and tried not to smile.

'Mummy, I was frightened, and I hung on to Mutton—'

'I threw a snowball,' said her brother.

'Yes, it hit me, then Mutton got loose and chased it away through the hedge.'

'I think you've both been very brave,' said their mother. 'They were chased by an imp,' she told me solemnly, 'like they see in their comic. And you deserve another cake,' she told her children.

'*And* Mutton!' cried the little girl.

'He shall have a piece of liver from the butcher's.'

And that was that.

A day or two later, Jamie came into the kitchen and dropped his schoolbag.

'Dad,' he said above the rattle of the potato peeler. I stopped the potato peeler. 'Guess what, Dad.'

I lowered my chin, waiting.

'You know how Miss Coulter likes telling stories?'

'Mm.'

'You know how it was raining last night? Right?'

'Ri-ight.'

'And you know that Miss Coulter lives in a flat in the top floor of the school?'

'Mm.'

'And you know how the rain was really loud—'

I nodded.

'—and it woke Miss Coulter?'

'Did it?'

'Well, she got up, and looked out of her bedroom window into the playground. You know how the little kids play peevers under the elm tree? And how the earth's worn into a hollow? There's always a puddle there. Well, Miss Coulter said the puddle was bigger than she'd ever seen it with the rain bouncing in it. She can see because of the lamp post outside the school gate. Even through her window she could hear the rain battering on the leaves of the tree – not that there are many leaves left at this time of year – but battering so that the tree shook—'

The kitchen door bumped open and Josie charged in, threw her schoolbag on the floor and hauled open the fridge door.

Our silence made her turn round.

'Sorry.' She lifted a block of square sausage from the fridge and sliced quietly.

'Do me one, Josie,' said Jamie. 'She said it was really spooky, 'cos the raindrops glittered in the light from the lamp post, and nobody was about. All the village, she said, was in its night's sleep. Then—'

Sausage fizzled on the hot plate.

'—she saw somebody under the tree.'

'I thought she was looking down from her window?' I said. 'How could she see under the tree?'

'Dad. It's a Camperdown Elm. Not a great huge elm. It's little and twisted, and she could see between the branches because there were hardly any leaves. I told you that.'

'Sorry.'

'—under the tree.' Jamie paused dramatically.

'What does under the tree mean?' asked Josie, finding a bag of bread to stick her hand in. She pulled out four slices.

'Miss Coulter saw somebody under the tree!' groaned Jamie. 'Do you want me to tell this, or not?'

'Oh, get on!'

Jamie pulled his face into the mood, and got on.

'She thought somebody was sheltering from the rain. Then she wondered who could be out at this time of night because it was three o'clock in the morning.

'Then she saw more than one person, but she couldn't make out if they were children or grown-ups. They seemed small for grown-ups, and if they *were* children – she thought – what were they doing out in the middle of the night? And – she thought – if they were *grown-ups* what were *they* doing out in the middle of the night!'

Josie flipped the sausage over on the hot plate and it sizzled loudly.

'One of the people crept from under the tree with its hand out to feel the rain. Now, guess what, Dad? Miss Coulter said this simple act gave her the creeps.

'She said it just wasn't the way a person would feel the rain – you know – with your palm up. She said it was feeling it more the way you milk a cow. Then another person crept from under the tree and felt the rain with its finger and thumb.

'Miss Coulter said the street light caught the finger and thumb just so, so she could see it. Then the rest came out and walked around the puddle as if they'd never seen a puddle before. One walked into it not noticing, she thought, and leapt out again, and she heard its voice. She'd been thinking they were children because of the way they were behaving, but that voice, she said, was too harsh. More like a crow, she said, than a person, and it made her shiver, though she pretended to herself that the shiver was because of the cold, but . . .

'Anyway. Miss Coulter began to make out their clothes. Remember these devils, Dad? Well, the way Miss Coulter described the clothes reminded me of *them!*

'Then, guess what? The one that had walked into

the puddle walked in again! Miss Coulter said the others seemed to get courage from this and they went in, wading, then stamping, then slapping the water with their hands, then kneeling in it, and before she knew it, the puddle was full of these people dancing in the water, rolling in it and shrieking with laughter.

'That's what scared her, Dad. That laughter. She was so scared she said that she threw her window open and yelled at them to go home to their beds. And you know how Miss Coulter can yell.

'They huddled – still in the water, clothes soaking – she thought she could see them shivering but not bothering about being cold – then they looked up and she saw every bony little face staring at her until her heart beat so fast she thought she would faint. Then they ran out of the gate and along the road.

'Miss Coulter said she thought they were pretending to run away. I mean, they really ran, but she thought they could just as easily have come into the school and got her, only they decided otherwise. Luckily for her. She actually phoned the police and Brian said he would—'

'Frances's Brian?' asked Josie, toppling sausage between slices of bread. She passed one sandwich to Jamie.

'Thanks. Interesting, eh, Dad?'

'Hmm,' I said.

And I meant it.

'Well, that's nothing,' said Josie munching. 'Andrew MacAndrew, who's thick like porridge in a drawer, *he* saw . . .'

I didn't hear what Andrew MacAndrew saw. I bumped out of the kitchen and found Frances.

I said, 'Frances, get Brian round here. Go on.'

Then I caught Esther's eye, and I knew that she knew the business with the devils had started again.

My Esther could read all that in my face.

And she was right.

16

Brian yawned into my restaurant, wearing his jumper.

I was wearing my blazer and eating my fish and chip lunch.

'You took your time,' I said. 'Sit down. Coffee?'

Brian sat and yawned.

'Please. I've been run off my feet these last few weeks. Clothing pinched off washing lines all over the place. The washing lines pinched too. And junk food. I don't know. And I was on duty last night. I should still be asleep, but Frances nagged me into seeing you—'

'The devils are back.'

Brian stopped yawning.

Frances brought his coffee, and put her hand on his shoulder.

My glance pushed her away.

'We need action,' I said, eating my fish.

Something in the way Brian gulped his coffee made me pause – as if drinking coffee were more important than devils.

'What's wrong?' I demanded.

'Mm?'

'What's up?' I chewed.

'With me?'

'With you.'

'Nothing.'

I put a glint in my eye, but Brian avoided it by beckoning Frances.

'Scrambled egg, please, Frances.' Frances turned away.

Brian beamed at me like an idiot. 'Good coffee. What were you saying, Allan? Devils? Ho, ho, ho.'

'Ho, ho, ho?'

'Well, I mean to say. Devils.' Brian was shaking

his head as if I had mentioned fairies in the rhubarb.

'Your inspector,' I reminded Brian, 'and Dr Alexander took away the devil in the jar—'

'Ah, no. They didn't.'

Brian blushed.

'They didn't?' I repeated quietly.

Brian shrugged and looked around the restaurant for spies. 'It's still in Rose Cottage.'

'What!'

'I've been sworn to secrecy.'

'Tell me!' I demanded.

'People mustn't know. Panic, and all that. You were asked to keep quiet, weren't you? Think of the outcry. What action would the government take?'

'*I* don't know!'

'I'm not *asking* you,' said Brian. 'That's what *people* would ask. Think of the turmoil if it got out that devils existed. Like I said, panic.'

'So why is the devil still in Rose Cottage?'

Brian shrugged. 'They can't decide what to do for the best.'

I understood now why Mrs Patience was still with Lenny in the council house. She wouldn't be allowed back to Rose Cottage until Somebody made a decision.

'Well,' I said, 'somebody must make a decision . . .'

Brian was shaking his head.

'. . . because a woman fell over a paving stone outside Rose Cottage. I looked at the pavement, Brian. It's sinking. I would say that devils have dug a hole underneath it again. And an imp chased two kids across a field. And you investigated Miss Coulter's story about people in the playground. Face it, Brian!' I hissed, as his head shook faster. 'They're back! Do you really want more and more devils roaming the village? Are you going down in history, Brian, as the police officer who let devils into the world? Because that's what's happening. Stealing clothes – like they did before. Stealing rope – for some reason. And junk food. YOU CAN BE A WIMP IF YOU LIKE,' I said loudly so that Frances, approaching with Brian's scrambled egg, looked up sharply, 'or,' I said quietly, 'you can come with me to Rose Cottage after dark – tonight.'

The clear black sky above the village was broken with stars. Lights shone from house windows, but the streets stretched cold and empty.

I crept round the side of Rose Cottage.

Dead leaves leapt from my toes with a damp, nervous whispering.

I was glad to step on to the quiet lawn at the back of the house.

In the starlight I could make out the windows standing flat and black.

'Brian?' I said.

A blob rose from behind a dustbin. 'Here.'

I jumped. 'Oh, my heart!' I whispered.

'Sorry. I was early. Walked my beat too fast. We shouldn't be doing this. Does Esther know?'

'She's asleep. Shine your torch on the lock.' Our two torches wobbled on the back door of Rose

Cottage steadying on the keyhole.

I slid in the key.

It wouldn't turn.

I tried the handle, and the door opened.

'It wasn't locked,' I whispered.

We looked at each other above the torches.

Brian knew I'd got the key from Mrs Patience. And I knew that a spare key had been left in the sideboard drawer – where anybody popping up from the cellar, I thought, could find it.

'I'll switch on the kitchen light,' I whispered. After all, we weren't burglars.

But the light didn't come on.

'Electricity's off,' said Brian.

We moved our ovals of torchlight around the kitchen and bugs ran away from crumbs.

'Bit of a mess,' said Brian.

Mrs Patience, I knew, wouldn't have left a mess.

We stepped among crisp bags into the hall. A mouse fled squeaking from a scatter of biscuits.

I whispered, 'Junk food,' remembering Brian

mentioning that junk food had been stolen from the village shops.

We wavered the torches across the hall and down the cellar steps. The cellar door was shut.

I could hear my own breathing.

I eased one foot down the first step.

'Come on,' I breathed, and descended the second step.

I realised that Brian wasn't following.

'Come *on!*' I hissed.

'I heard something,' said Brian.

'No, you didn't!'

'Listen!'

I sighed. Heard something, indeed. He was scared.

Then I heard something too.

Not in the cellar, but behind me; sneaking through Mrs Patience's kitchen.

17

My heart bounced like a pickled egg.

I stared back towards the kitchen, forgetting to point my torch, so that I was staring into darkness with only the faint shape of the kitchen doorway to look at. A small figure that seemed familiar moved into the doorway.

Really, I didn't want to meet a devil that wasn't shut in a jar.

But the figure wasn't a devil.

It said, 'Wait till I find the main switch.'

I blew my breath out with relief because the voice belonged to Mrs Patience, though I couldn't see who she was talking to. She heard me, and snapped, 'Is that you, Allan Henderson?'

'It's me,' I assured her. 'And Brian. When you

gave me the back door key you promised to let me handle this! Is that Lenny ... Leonard ... with you?'

'Hello, Allan,' said Leonard, and his voice was too loud in this darkness. 'We found Frances in the street,' he said.

'Frances!' said Brian. And Frances's shape appeared in the doorway.

She fumbled towards Brian. 'I wanted to say good night,' she murmured. 'I knew you'd be on your beat near here—'

'Frances!'

'—and when I saw Allan sneaking round the back of the cottage—'

'Sneaking?' I said.

'—I knew you were nearby because I overheard you arranging this when I served your scrambled egg—'

'Oh, Frances,' sighed Brian.

The light came on – though dimly, for the bulb in the hall was small. Mrs Patience straightened up from the cupboard which contained the main electric switch.

'Mrs Patience,' I said, and stood firmly between the old lady and the staircase.

She said: 'Allan Henderson, this is my cottage—'

But before I could argue, voices floated in from the back door, and in came Jamie and Josie whispering like criminals, and Esther looking beautiful but uncombed, and demanding to know why I wasn't in my bed – she had heard me going out, and the children had wakened, and just what was going on, don't you know you have a restaurant to run in the morning, and some of us need our sleep even if you don't?

'Right. Right-right-right,' I said.

And Brian said, 'It's all right.'

Esther quietened down, and I explained that I wanted to find out what the devils were up to, and would they all mind leaving?

But Frances clung to Brian, Mrs Patience nailed me with her eye; Esther almost smiled proudly,

133

thinking – I suppose – that I was being brave, and announced she would stay. And Josie and Jamie wanted to be first into the cellar.

Only Leonard looked longingly towards the kitchen and the freedom of the night outside; and I wondered if Mrs Patience had persuaded him to come, or if he'd been strong enough to put his fear of the hole aside; and I saw that he had put his fear aside, for I noticed his hand close on his mother's, engulfing it gently but strongly.

And I was pleased. Whatever Leonard had experienced that had knocked the wits out of him, he was fighting it.

'Well,' I said, looking round the waiting faces of my family and friends. 'Let's get on.'

So we did.

We got on.

We faced the staircase to the cellar.

Brian hesitated. Jamie and Josie dashed in front of me, and I collared them and passed them back to Esther. I trotted down the steps and reached for the handle of the cellar door. I looked back up the stairs.

Brian had his arms around Frances.

Behind Esther and the children, Lenny . . . Leonard . . . towered beside his mother, peering anxiously.

I said, 'You don't have to come, Leonard. There may be nothing at all down here—'

Mrs Patience opened her mouth sharply, and I raised my palm in surrender.

Right. I grasped the handle and pushed open the cellar door. Little of the dim light reached down from the hall, so I flashed my torch into darkness; but the dimness from the hall sprayed confusingly amid the bouncing torchlight, and it seemed for a second that a flurry of movement disturbed the shadows in the cellar – like upstairs in the kitchen when the bugs had hurried from the crumbs.

But not bugs.

Bigger things than bugs.

And the movement was muffled, as if the cellar

was carpeted, rather than having an earthen floor; and my torch crept across the floor, and I bent to stare, for I saw a shirt tied to trousers; and tied to the trousers, a rope; and a jumper knotted to a skirt; and more rope, clothes and rope heaped deep in tangled masses of colour, each piece tied to another; and I shone the torch over the heaps, and I saw gate posts, ten resting on the lawnmower and a dozen propped against the cardboard box, all dark, with carved heads instead of knobbly tops.

Then Brian leant on my shoulder and Frances's small hand pressed my back as she whispered, 'Don't push!' but Jamie and Josie pushed so that everybody's weight came on me, and I staggered through the doorway.

Mrs Patience cried, 'Switch on that cellar light!' But my legs gave way, and I fell on my torch and the bodies flattened me, Frances's hair landing in my mouth, and I heard a crack and feared I'd broken a rib against the torch.

Esther's feet pattered down the few steps. She

said, 'Are you all right? Are you hurt? The light won't work.'

Then the bodies came off me, letting me breathe, and the only casualty was Brian whose brow had hit the cellar's light bulb, smashing it (which was the crack I heard) and leaving a line of blood for Frances to wipe from his eye.

'You all right, Allan?' Leonard's hands lifted me clear of the floor so that I dangled for a moment, my shoulders against the ceiling.

'Thanks, Leonard. I landed on these clothes. Look at them all. You didn't put these here, Mrs Patience?'

I shone the torch on her and she waved the light away as she shook her head at such a suggestion.

Then I remembered the gate posts.

And I remembered the flurry of movement when I opened the cellar door; and I said, 'Ssh!' making everyone stop, and I turned my torch towards the walls.

Brian pointed his torch, and together we spotlighted a group of gate posts.

The carved heads were frozen in the light and the bodies leaned rigid. Knee-deep around the posts rose the piles of tied clothes and rope.

And so we shone the torches, and held our breaths.

Oh, I knew what we were seeing, but I didn't understand: Devils as still as gate posts, and miles of clothes and rope.

Miles.

Long enough, I thought, to dangle to the centre of the earth, and strong enough, I thought, to (maybe!) pull up something that couldn't climb the rough sides of the hole – and since the devils *could* climb, then what I wondered – my breath snatching fast gasps as my heart speeded up – what *were* they pulling up out of the hole? What were they bringing up from the hot, black interior of the planet into our village?

What *could* they be bringing up?

Suddenly, I'd had enough.

I turned to the others.

'Get out of here!' I yelled.

18

I think every one of us knew that the gate posts were the devils; devils standing still, as some animals stand still when they are visible; for at my yell we fled for the stairs, myself last, because I was farthest into the cellar.

I pulled the door closed, my heart pulsing, but I clung to the door rather than running up the stairs; and I gasped, 'Wait!

'Wait!' I panted, and the others paused in their flight, staring under the hall light as if I was mad. I could see in every face the question: Do we run or stay?

'We came to fix those devils,' I whispered.

'Dad's right,' gulped Jamie.

'I wasn't running away,' said Josie. 'You said to get out—'

'Not now, Josie! Suggestions? Brian?'

Brian frowned, panting.

'Esther? Mrs Patience? Frances? Somebody!'

'Let's throw them down the hole,' said Leonard, and everybody looked at him.

He swayed with embarrassment.

'It won't hurt them,' he said. 'I've been down. Haven't I?' He appealed to his mother, and she nodded.

'I thought,' said Leonard hesitantly, 'that it was maybe a nightmare. I dream about it, you know. I dream every night that I'm falling. Not landing. And I'm climbing. I've got words in my head.'

He leaned down to his mother at his side.

He whispered, *'Don't think. Climb. Don't stop.* These words are in my head now when I wake up, and when I go to sleep. I never told anyone, Mum. Nobody would have believed I'd climbed all that way in the darkness. *Don't think. Climb. Don't stop.* Up I came. Climb. I didn't think. Up. I didn't stop. Up I climbed, Mum. Allan, up I came. *Don't think.*

Climb. Don't stop. Up and up. But I've thought about it.

'I thought about it in hospital. I must have climbed for days. But I don't know how. No food. Up. *Don't think—*'

'Leonard!' I said.

He breathed fast.

'Leonard, it wasn't a dream,' I assured him. 'You did climb. You climbed better than anyone ever climbed. Ever.'

He looked at me seriously.

I said, 'I mean it. I'm not exaggerating. You fell down the hole. How you survived landing, I don't know. Maybe you'll remember one day. It doesn't matter. What matters is that you climbed out.'

'I climbed out,' whispered Leonard, and something in his face changed, and I saw understanding in his eyes; and he looked at Brian and Frances as if seeing them as a couple in love, and knowing this. And he looked at Esther and knew she was a woman; and at Jamie and

Josie, and he began a smile as he saw they were kids; then he turned to his mum, and his smile opened into a beam that shone brighter than any electric light, and he swamped Mrs Patience in an embrace that could have gathered up the universe.

Then he released her, and he said, 'Mum?'

Mrs Patience crinkled her face to shut in her tears, but she couldn't. The tears leaked down her cheeks.

She said, 'Son.'

Leonard said, 'I remember now. My Dad . . . Oh, I've been a fool. I've been out of my head. Allan? Esther? Eating bacon rolls and drinking tea all these years . . .'

He stood to his full great height and filled his chest with air. His voice rang out (but no longer booming): 'I AM LEONARD PATIENCE, SON OF AGNES PATIENCE, SON OF JIMMY PATIENCE, AND I AM – A – MAN!'

He held his breath for long seconds, then he

relaxed, and his mother clung to him, and wept, and Frances wept, and Josie wept.

And we waited, Brian, Jamie, Esther and I, watching the final healing: the return of a son to his mother.

Then we relaxed too, and for a moment, I thought Esther was going to offer to make us tea, but behind me, through the cellar door, I heard movement, and held up my hand.

We listened, Mrs Patience's old eyes glancing up at Leonard's face as if unable to believe that he was normal again; and cackles of hair-raising laughter whispered behind the cellar door, and 'Oomph!' quietly, then 'Oomph!' again, the devils' voices making a song almost, and I half-expected one voice raised above the 'Oomph!' to sing the melody; but the 'Oomph!' throbbed on, and I realised what the devils were doing.

I whispered, 'Put out the light!' And out went the hall light.

Brian switched on his torch.

'No,' I said. 'Switch it off.' And in darkness we listened to the continuing 'Oomph!'

In the darkness I waited until my eyes began to see the faint shape, again, of the kitchen doorway; then, slowly, I turned the handle of the cellar door, and pushed.

I pushed the door wider so that the 'Oomph!' throbbed out of the darkness; and I sensed the movement of the devils in the cellar; perhaps I smelled the mothballs yet, and certainly I smelled the smell you get in any clothes shop, and even the stringy scent of the rope reached my nostrils, and a faint acid pong which I assumed came from so many devils working together.

Working at what? Was I right, that they were pulling something out of the hole?

If I was right, should we stop them? or should we make contact with the thing in the hole as if greeting an alien from another galaxy?

Should we call the fire brigade?

I could see nothing, for the darkness was almost complete.

And because I could see nothing, I could not decide what to do.

And as I hesitated, it seemed that the darkness lightened, and I knew that my eyes were opening wider to soak in what little starlight was reaching from the kitchen down to the cellar.

I saw the bulk of the devils in a group, and the group leaned at the sound of 'Oomph!' Then again 'Oomph!' and other groups leaned; and near the door, close to my feet where the darkness was less dark, clothing and rope piled up slowly with each pull; for I was right; I was right that the devils had tied clothes and ropes into long, long lengths, and that these lengths hung down into the hole beyond the cellar wall – for the wall had been taken down, and the earth cleared away above the hole again, leaving a little cave again – and I was right that the devils were pulling something up from below; something heavy. Something, I discovered at that moment, which R O A R E D with a voice that blasted past me up the staircase and rattled the windows in Mrs Patience's kitchen.

19

Although the windows rattled, the roar was still far down the hole, but the 'Oomph!' certainly speeded up as if obeying a command.

I tried to think.

Brian shifted restlessly. I sensed he wanted to get away and find help.

But there was no time.

Whatever had to be done, we had to do.

And whatever that is, I told myself, I might as well be able to see. So I felt past Brian. Frances's hair streamed between my fingers. I found a small shoulder. I didn't know if it was Josie or Jamie. I felt higher and caught hold of an ear. I pulled it close and breathed directly into it: 'Give me the light bulb out of the hall. Tell Leonard.'

The ear nodded.

'Oomph!'

Something smooth touched my cheek and I reached up and small fingers released the light bulb into my hand.

I put my torch in my pocket and stepped into the cellar on to the silent piled-up clothes.

Devils 'Oomphed!' around me. The cellar ceiling was against the back of my bent head.

I felt around the ceiling and found the socket with the razor-edged remains of the original bulb waiting to slice my fingers.

I gritted my teeth, found a grip on the metal base of the bulb and removed it from the socket. I dropped it on the clothes at my ankles, and pushed in the bulb from the hall – my heart jumping, for I didn't know if the bulb would light, because I didn't know if the switch was on or off.

The bulb didn't light.

I stepped back.

'Oomph!'

I found the light switch.

'Oomph!'

I took a long breath—

'Oomph!'

—and switched on.

The devils didn't blink.

'Oomph!'

They pulled the lengths of clothing.

'Oomph!'

The clothing and rope had gathered high around the cellar walls. The lengths the devils were pulling, vanished tautly into the hole inside the low cave of earth.

'Oomph!'

'Stop!' I said.

I didn't know what else to do.

'Stop!' I shouted, and the others joined in. 'Stop! Stop!' But the devils pulled and oomphed.

'Dad?' squeaked Jamie.

'Brian?' I asked hopefully. But Brian was useless,

just as I was. Then it was too late.

Josie pointed towards the hole.

The 'Oomph!' slowed.

Something leapt out of the hole and landed on the earth right at the hole's edge, and cold horror slid down my back; another something, resembling the first something, clung to the earth, and I recognized the gigantic black hands which belonged to the picture in Mrs Patience's book.

'Agjam!' I whispered, then with one final 'Oomph' up in a rush shot the rest of the creature.

Oh.

It was gigantic.

It crawled from the hole, its back scraping the roof of the low cave so that earth fell among its spines. It had crawled from a platform of wood which had the clothing tied to it. It stood up into the dim brightness of the cellar but still it was bent almost double, the spines on its back scratching the ceiling. It stayed still, panting, I thought, for it seemed to breathe like a man, the spines glittering

151

on its shoulders, glittering on its head; and its single round eye in the middle of its face caught the light, bouncing a dazzling arrow around the cellar.

And – as in the picture – the face was black and blank.

I felt Frances sag into a heap beside me.

Esther was whispering, 'Do something! Do something!' over and over. But I didn't know what to do.

A small hand crept into mine. Two small hands crept up my arm. I couldn't take my eyes off Agjam.

The small hand pulled, making me lean over.

'Dad,' whispered Jamie. 'In the cave. Where that thing's spikes scraped away the earth. I can see the workman's shovel.'

Workman's shovel?

It meant nothing.

Why was my son telling me about a shovel when, for all I knew, the world was about to end?

But I looked past Agjam and saw the blade of the shovel sticking down from the roof of the cave, and all the time, Esther was whispering, 'Do something! Do something before it's too late!'

Then Jamie whispered, 'It's right above the hole, Dad. Pull the shovel down . . .'

Then I saw what he meant.

Pull the shovel down.

Oh, what a child!

Pull the shovel down. I saw exactly what my wonderful intelligent son meant. I looked at the devils still clinging to the ropes. I had to pull the shovel down . . .

For a second I remembered that the shovel had fallen deep into the hole past the workman's chest, but I guessed the devils had brought it up again to dig with, and had left it jammed in the earth, perhaps to support the roof of the cave . . . ?

Pull the shovel down.

But Agjam was between me and the hole.

Trembling, I stepped closer to the monstrous creature.

The round eye wobbled at me.

'I'm Jamie!' squeaked Jamie behind me, and the eye shone at him. I risked another step.

'This is my sister, Josie!'

I stepped on a devil's tail but it only slid me a dirty look.

'And this is my Mum! She runs a restaurant! Really good food! Chips. Pizzas . . .'

I squeezed between devils, stepping over the lengths of clothing which they still held, which were still attached to the wooden platform. Four paces would take me into the cave.

'. . . and Frances is our waitress. Brian's her boyfriend. He's the local booby – I mean bobby. Watch out for him. Ha. Ha. Ha. And this . . .'

I ran – suddenly – desperately – staggering over the heaps of clothing. I threw myself under the low roof of the cave landing on my back beside the hole, and I grabbed the sticking-down blade of the shovel – and pulled.

I couldn't have wished for better.

The shovel came down in my hands. Earth broke

away from the cave roof. The roof roared. I rolled back into the cellar. Concrete slabs from the pavement above crashed on to the wooden platform which the devils had pulled up from below.

When the earth and slabs hit the platform, the platform sank under the tremendous weight, its ropes of clothes sliding into the hole – and the devils instinctively held on.

Dust exploded through the cellar.

Agjam turned, his spines scratching the roof, but he seemed too startled to help the devils or to order them to let go the ropes, and the weight of the collapsing pavement was truly enormous, so that no matter how the devils hung on, no matter how they fumed and cried out, the ropes slid faster into the hole, dragging the devils across the floor until the first of them popped down into the dusty emptiness.

Then more and more devils slid, tumbling and shrieking and fuming over the earthy edge until the last of them was yanked away, their voices fading, and only the vast piles of clothing and ropes were left flowing after them, down into the dusty emptinesses within our planet.

Until, at last, there was nothing around our feet but the cellar floor, and before us – standing in a fog of dust which swirled with the fresh night air which flowed in from outside where the pavement had vanished – loomed the dreadful figure of the gigantic Agjam.

And what we could do about him, I hadn't a clue.

20

But Leonard knew what to do about Agjam.

Leonard stepped in front of my family and friends. He was bent double like Agjam, under the ceiling. I guessed they were about the same height.

And I saw that they were the same massive build. Leonard was as strong as four navvies.

How strong, I wondered, was the demon?

And those spikes, I observed, were jolly dangerous.

I glanced at the hole.

The dust had cleared enough for me to see. The hole was directly behind Agjam with nothing but darkness of night above it, and the darkness of emptiness inside it.

Leonard crouched.

Agjam growled.

I frowned as I stared at Agjam.

Those fingers really did look like rubber tyres.

And the spikes on his head and shoulders – they really did look like spokes from a bicycle.

Very strange.

Very –

Leonard ran at Agjam.

Agjam staggered back, growling in surprise. His monstrous hands landed on Leonard's shoulders and pushed.

Leonard pushed back.

I wondered why Agjam didn't grab Leonard's throat, or shoulder him with the spikes.

They swayed, two giants in the dusty light, scraping their backs on the ceiling.

'Get him, Lenny!' screamed Josie, and Agjam froze.

'Tear his head off, Leonard!' shouted Frances who had long since risen from her faint.

Agjam still didn't move. Leonard heaved him

towards the hole, and the demon's foot touched emptiness, though he still held Leonard's shoulders, and—

Something wasn't right.

Agjam wasn't fighting like a demon at all.

He wasn't fighting.

Leonard drew back his fist. One blow and Agjam would be gone.

One blow, I thought, and down would go Agjam back to where he'd come from.

One—

The demon's single eye flickered into Leonard's face.

Leonard's fist hesitated.

Agjam withdrew its foot from the hole and took its hands from Leonard's shoulders. It tilted its head as it stood bent beneath the ceiling, to look at each one of us.

Then – it spoke.

It said, 'L e o n a r d?'

We gaped.

I can see them yet, the two giants, one black and glittering on the brink of the hole, the other brave and young. And Esther with her mouth open and the kids in a numb crouch; and Frances and Brian clinging to each other, dumbfounded at Leonard's name coming from the monster's mouth.

Though it had no mouth.

'Leonard?' it said again.

I saw the black flap that was the face move, as if breath had pushed it from inside.

And Leonard lowered his fist. His fingers touched the flap and pulled it gently aside, and the single eye came away with the flap, and beneath was the face of a man.

'Leonard?' croaked the man. 'Are you my Leonard? Are you my baby boy?'

And Leonard stepped back.

Mrs Patience stumbled forward, her eyes huge with staring. Tears ran silent and wondering down her old cheeks.

She said, 'Jimmy?'

'Agnes?' whispered the demon. 'Agnes? Is it you? Agnes. Agnes. Leonard. Agnes! Leonard! I'm your Dad, Leonard! Agnes, I've come home, my lassie!'

I can't hope to describe what we felt.

What Mrs Patience felt, I will never know. And what Leonard felt is beyond imagining. I wondered if the shock would scatter his wits again.

But it didn't.

Weeks went by, and we had a new family visiting the restaurant: Mr and Mrs Jimmy Patience and their son Leonard.

How they talked.

How we listened.

I, certainly, listened.

When Leonard and his Dad first fell together down the hole, they survived because of – quite simply – a tremendous updraught of air caused by natural heat inside the earth. The air in other words, acted like a cushion so that they landed with only a good bruising.

And Leonard survived the prodigious climb out again, because Jimmy spent a long time making him repeat the words that had stuck in his head: Don't think. Climb. Don't stop.

Leonard's great strength and stamina, even when he was eight, plus his faith in his Dad, brought him to the top of the hole. And food, it seemed, was no problem.

'You won't remember this, Leonard,' growled his father in his unused voice, 'but down there so far deep in the ground, there is nothing. No food, and no need of food. No need of air, even – though there was air. That is Hell, my friends,' said Jimmy, as I poured him more tea. 'Possessing nothing and doing nothing. Creating nothing. Having no hope of change or achievement. No night and no day, no varying seasons. One moment is like every other moment. One year is like every other year; except there are no years and no moments. I had no idea how long I kept Leonard with me, feeding his mind with those thoughts that just might get him home.

'And I have no idea how long I took persuading the devils to come to the surface. Normally, devils only appear in this world if some fool conjures them up; but I knew that the vent was there – the hole is a volcanic vent–'

'Oh, is it?' I said.

'–and of course I knew it was there because I'd fallen down it.' And Jimmy laughed till the windows in my restaurant rattled.

'But I talked the devils into coming to the surface. You see, they are dull creatures, naturally, living where they do. But I had my pack of cards on me, and various little tricky things, so I showed them tricks and invented tricks, and talked about this world and focused their minds on food until eventually – how long? – decades, oh, decades, how hard to believe it took all that time! But decades it took to catch their interest, enough for them to make the effort to climb to the surface.

'Go, I told them, and find food! Enjoy yourselves! For you see, if *they* got out, perhaps *I* could get out.

163

Perhaps I could persuade them that they needed me with them, for – you understand – I couldn't climb out of the hole. It was too far for me. I wasn't light enough, and I wasn't young enough, like Leonard, to believe that I could do it.

'Then they brought the wheelchair. Oh, that was an occasion! That was my miracle! My friends that wheelchair was my salvation, for you see, I remembered my little Latin book. The wheelchair reminded me of one picture in the book, with words of prophecy saying that Agjam would lead the devils to freedom to experience the delights of the human world.

'And so I took the wheelchair to pieces – what a lot of work! What labour! What fun and interest! And I transformed myself into Agjam-with-the-single-eye that looked to the future.

'Single eye, my foot! The lens of the torch – the torch that fell down with a great length of string attached to it the same day (I think!) that Leonard and I fell down! That – eventually – was my eye!

Ha! Ha! Oh, I made those devils do my bidding then! I told them that the two devils I had conjured up must be returned!

'They must be returned to Hell! or people would find them, and find out all about devils and come down and destroy them, every one! And the poor dim things believed me, thinking I was their great lord Agjam (which – oh! ho! ho! ho! is part of Agnes's name and part of my name! Agnes and James. Ha! ha! ha!) Oh, oh dear, but, of course, I never told the devils where their two friends were. I never said one was in a jar in a cardboard box. And I didn't know myself what had become of the one that Leonard had hammered.

'Then, of course! when they found the dead devil and slipped him away from under the pavement but failed to find the devil in the jar, I raged and fumed and ordered them to take me up into this world. Oh. I remembered the old tallboy and told them to drop that down, and down it dropped, slowing on the cushioning air, and of course nobody missed it because Rose Cottage was deserted! which was lucky for me! Then the devils stole clothes and ropes and tied them together until we had huge lengths long enough to reach down and tie to the tallboy. And the tallboy was my platform, and up I came. Oh, up. And I must say I didn't recognise any one of you in the cellar, but you were real people, and oh! I just looked and looked, and I couldn't speak for joy!

'And you know, I was astounded when this great hulk of a man attacked me! I didn't understand at first! Then I remembered that I was dressed as Agjam! Ah! Ha! Ha! Ha! Ha! Ha! Oh, dear! Oh! And then someone spoke his name . . .

'Oh, what a relief to be home.

'Oh, my Leonard, and my Agnes!

'Home.

'I am home.

'I am really, really home.'

166

Last Word

Now and then I remember things which need explanation. I don't want to go into details of who said what; but the devil in the jar, of course, had to go. We did that almost straight away after Agjam turned into Jimmy Patience.

We tipped the jar up and unclipped its stopper in the cellar, and gin ran over the floor and down the hole (which was open to the sky after the pavement falling in); and we helped the devil to its feet, and it staggered around, drunk as a weasel and eventually toppled headfirst into the hole and vanished with no more than a hiccup.

The hole itself was blocked eventually with a ten-ton concrete cork, and the pavement filled in over it.

You'll remember that the dead devil was originally in the magic circle, and that Mrs Patience had left the cellar to make a piece-and-jam for Leonard while Jimmy worried about how to get the devil-in-the-jar into the circle. At that time nobody knew about the hole. The cellar wall had not been disturbed then.

Well.

The devil in the circle was smarter than your usual devil, and talked at Jimmy while he was trying to think; it didn't talk sense, he said, but rambled on about all sorts of dull things (being dull brutes with nothing to do) and it mentioned amid its ramblings, the hole.

The hole had been there—

'Where?' Jimmy had demanded.

—for millions of years. Even the oldest devils couldn't remember when the hole wasn't there; but none of them had thought of a use for it, but maybe there was a use for it now; maybe the other devil (in the jar – though the chatting devil didn't know where it was) could be lowered down the hole instead of having to be put in the magic circle.

That made Jimmy haul the cellar wall apart, and hack out a gap in the earth under the pavement until he found the hole – which the devil promptly pushed him into.

You know what happened next – Jimmy fell down the hole taking wee Leonard with him, and the devil was left with his head bashed in.

One detail concerns the wheelchair. You know what hospitals are like – they treat people like invalids. The ambulance that eventually took Lenny to hospital when he was a boy, brought a wheelchair for him, but he didn't need it and wouldn't use it, and he caused a commotion during which the wheelchair got left at Rose Cottage. And where do you put a wheelchair you don't need?

. . . In the cellar – where the devils found it the day they came to eat in my restaurant. I must say that I never wondered where the wheelchair had come from or where it vanished to after the devils stopped using it; though, of course, they took it with them down the hole and gave it to Jimmy.

Well.

That's about it.

Except that my kids don't say I'm thick any more.

Excuse me, Jamie's trying to tell me something.

'Paid? Good. It's only been months. You did thank him anyway, son?'

That was Jamie telling me that the last of the workmen has just paid for the meal he had the day this adventure started.

I may say, the only policeman who's paid so far is Brian. No choice, I suppose, now he's engaged to Frances.

Here's Esther to take over the kitchen while I have my lunch. I'll slip my blazer on. I wonder if Mrs Patience is in the restaurant with Leonard and Jimmy. Nice people. Though why they named their house Rose Cottage, I'll never understand.

I mean, Rose Cottage! Can you really credit any sensible man calling his home . . . !

Another Hodder Children's book

THE GRAVE-DIGGER

Hugh Scott

What secrets lie buried . . . ?

Abernetha's grandfather is a grave-digger. She knows all his stories, but this one is true. Who is the mysterious figure in the graveyard? Could her grandfather have buried someone not quite dead? Together Abernetha and the grave-digger must confront the power of darkness, and destroy the evil that would turn a heart to stone . . .

ORDER FORM

0 340 68331 7	THE GRAVE-DIGGER *Hugh Scott*	£3.99	❐
0 340 65572 0	OWL LIGHT *Maggie Pearson*	£3.99	❐
0 340 68076 8	NIGHT PEOPLE *Maggie Pearson*	£3.99	❐
0 340 69371 1	THE BLOODING *Patricia Windsor*	£3.99	❐
0 340 68300 7	COMPANIONS OF THE NIGHT *Vivian Vande Velde*	£3.99	❐
0 340 68656 1	LOOK FOR ME BY MOONLIGHT *Mary Downing Hahn*	£3.99	❐
0 340 71031 4	THE BONE-DOG *Susan Price*	£3.99	❐

All Hodder Children's books are available at your local bookshop, or can be ordered direct from the publisher. Just tick the titles you would like and complete the details below. Prices and availability are subject to change without prior notice.

Please enclose a cheque or postal order made payable to *Bookpoint Ltd*, and send to: Hodder Children's Books, 39 Milton Park, Abingdon, OXON OX14 4TD, UK. Email Address: orders@bookpoint.co.uk

If you would prefer to pay by credit card, our call centre team would be delighted to take your order by telephone. Our direct line *01235 400414* (lines open 9.00 am–6.00 pm Monday to Saturday, 24 hour message answering service). Alternatively you can send a fax on *01235 400454*.

TITLE	FIRST NAME	SURNAME

ADDRESS	

DAYTIME TEL:	POST CODE

If you would prefer to pay by credit card, please complete:
Please debit my Visa/Access/Diner's Card/American Express (delete as applicable) card no:

Signature ....

Expiry Date: ....

If you would NOT like to receive further information on our products please tick the box. ❐